he moment Abe and Mitzy are swept back in time to the infamous Jack the Ripper murders, readers will clamor to find out what happens next."

—Anne Blankman, National Jewish Book Award-winning author of *The Blackbird Girls* and *Prisoner of Night and Fog*

"Vernick's clever use of a modern voice as foil for the Ripper's infamous murders perfectly complements the burgeoning friendship between time-displaced tweens amidst nineteenth century poverty and persecution."

—Dianne Salerni, author of *Eleanor, Alice, and the Roosevelt Ghosts*, a Jr. Library Guild Gold Standard selection

"*Ripped Away* is a rare, eye-opening novel that seamlessly blends fantasy, contemporary and historical fiction to illuminate the challenges teens face today with the horrors of the little-known blood libel brought upon London's East End Jews during the time of Jack the Ripper. It's a bold story few of us would ever know without Vernick's meticulous research, masterful storytelling, and her fierce determination to share truth and make sure that antisemitism is not omitted or erased from that history."

— Liza Wiemer, author of *The Assignment*, a 2021 Sydney Taylor Notable YA novel and 2021 YALSA Best Fiction for Young Adults

"*Ripped Away* is many things at once: a crackingly good, gaslit, time travel mystery packed with rich historical detail that also shines an important light on a lesser-known episode of anti-Semitism. This is the sort of book that makes lifelong readers out of reluctant ones."

— Jeff Zentner, Morris Award-winning author of *The Serpent King*

"Charming and inventive, *Ripped Away* transports the reader from modern-day America to the dark and dangerous of alleys of London during the terror reign of Jack the Ripper. It's *Back to the Future* through the eyes of young Abe Pearlman, a plucky, lovesick hero who doesn't realize that he's heroic."

—Steven Mayfield, Mari Sandoz Prize-winning author of *Treasure of the Blue Whale* and *Howling at the Moon*

"A time-bending, body-swapping, history-mystery, *Ripped Away* will have young readers eagerly turning pages."

—David Michael Slater, Montaigne Medal/Eric Hoffer Award finalist and author of *Forbidden Books* and *Sparks.*

RIPPED AWAY

Shirley Reva Vernick

Fitzroy Books

Published by Fitzroy Books
An imprint of
Regal House Publishing, LLC
Raleigh, NC 27587
All rights reserved

https://fitzroybooks.com

Printed in the United States of America

ISBN -13 (paperback): 9781646032037
ISBN -13 (epub): 9781646032044
Library of Congress Control Number: 2021936002

Interior and cover design by Lafayette & Greene
Cover images © by C.B. Royal

 Regal House Publishing, LLC
https://regalhousepublishing.com

Printed in the United States of America

In memory of Alice Rosen and Mickey Levine

1

Watch closely here, or you might miss what's going on.

See the guy walking out the school door? The one you could pick out from a lineup of Most Likely to Spend Saturday Night at Home? The one who keeps his head down, hands in his pockets, not exactly frowning but not looking delirious with life either? Yeah, that's me.

Notice that I'm not staying after for lacrosse practice or a soccer match. That's because, as my mom says, athletics are not my strong suit. Notice too that I'm not heading out with a pack of buddies. That's because, as my guidance counselor puts it, I'm a bit of a loner. Finally, notice that I'm not carrying any books. This is not because I'm a slacker. It's because, as my older sister points out, I'm the geek who takes photos of all my assigned pages, so I can read them off my phone anytime, anywhere. Just, you know, for lack of a real life.

Get the idea? Okay, now watch me walk out of the school building, past the Fort Pippin Regional Schools sign. Over by the parking lot, see the principal talking to the music teacher and one of the lunch ladies. Follow me as I mumble hello to the maintenance guy, then head up the foot path, nodding as I pass Mitzy Singer, who's sitting on the memorial bench. Lastly, tag along as I turn off the path, cut through the baseball field, and continue across Amity Street on my way into town.

There, I bet you missed it. You have no idea what the big deal is, am I right? Let's rewind. Cross back over Amity, go through the baseball field again, and onto the foot path. Stop at the memorial bench. There. Look at Mitzy Singer. The spiky blue hair, the wrist bangles, the cavalcade of ear studs, the black jeans. The restless dark eyes, the smile I know is hiding in there somewhere, the slight scent of rain. Go to the frame where I nod to her. Look what happens. Still not catching it? Then I'll have to explain it to you.

Nothing happens, that's what. Not even a snub. Not a single sign that she knows I'm alive. Which is what makes this a rotten day, right on top of all the other rotten days that came before, all the days when the blue-haired girl with the bewitching eyes looked right through me. It doesn't even matter that today is one of my favorite days of the year— National Elephant Appreciation Day, September 22. It's still lousy.

I first fell for Mitzy back in fourth grade, when our teacher Mrs. DuBray had the class create a 51st state, an island to be situated off the coast of North Carolina. We had to come up with a name for the state, its crops and industries, a flag, and a bunch of other stuff—including a state bird. The boys wanted it to be a raptor—a hawk or an owl or possibly a falcon, something that breakfasts on bunnies and chipmunks, not bugs and worms. The girls were more into plumage, so they wanted a peacock, a cardinal, maybe a toucan. All except Mitzy.

Mitzy raised her hand and said, "I think the state bird should be a Pegasus."

Which made the class erupt in laughter. Let me be clear here. They were laughing at her, not with her.

"Mitzy, dear," Mrs. DuBray said, "a Pegasus isn't a bird. It's a horse with wings."

"No," Mitzy told her, "a Pegasus is a bird with hoofs."

The class went silent.

As for me, I was a goner. It was the most twisted, non-sensical, perfect reasoning I'd ever heard. How could you not love a girl who could philosophize about taxonomy *and* muzzle a room full of kids, all in the space of eight words?

That day, I turned around and looked Mitzy straight in

her big brown eyes. But she looked right through me, just like she's done every day since. Not that she was, or is, singling me out for neglect. She's just that way. She's dreamy. Distracted. Faraway. She's Mitzy.

So today, like every other day, I nod to her, and she doesn't respond, and I daydream about how I wish it would go. How I'd slow down and say, "Hey, Mitzy," my tone cool, my hair perfect.

How she'd flush, a spray of pink freckles spreading across her cheeks. How I'd stand so close to her, our knees would almost touch, and I'd say, "Nice crescent moons."

How her hand would go to her new earrings, and the color in her cheeks would deepen. How she'd scoot over to make room for me on the bench. How she'd laugh a little, like a breeze, and it would be brilliant.

This is as far as my imagination brings me in the time it takes to walk past her, to have my hopes dashed yet again. Then I cut across the baseball field and head home.

There actually was one time, a couple of years ago, when Mitzy and I did interact. For two epic weeks, fate threw us together when Mr. Vasquez divided our science class into teams for—get this—the Battle of the Solar System. Each team got assigned a planet and had to come up with a ten-minute presentation. Mitzy, Wally Cruz, and I got Saturn, so we named ourselves the Titans after Saturn's biggest moon.

"You know what we need?" I told Mitzy and Wally the day before the presentation. "We need a logo."

"What for?" Mitzy asked. Her hair wasn't blue back then. It was light brown. And she only had a couple of studs in each ear.

"For our team," I said. "For the Titans. A big letter T or something."

"And that's supposed to get us a better grade?" Mitzy challenged.

"Maybe," I said. "Or maybe it'll, I don't know, give us

confidence. Or psych out the other teams." Mitzy just rolled her eyes. But the next morning she walked into school with a twelve-inch, fire-engine-red letter *T*. It was shiny and high-gloss and exactly what I'd been picturing.

At presentation time, we set our logo in front of the PowerPoint screen and made sure everyone knew the T was for Titans, for our team. It probably didn't improve our grade. It probably didn't psych out the other kids either. But it made me fall even harder for Mitzy, because maybe, just maybe, she liked the way I thought about things.

The story doesn't end there. A couple of days after that, I was riding my bike out on Route 9, and I nearly fell off my wheels when I passed the car wash. Because now instead of saying TOUCHLESS in fire-engine-red letters, the sign out front said OUCHLESS. Mitzy had nabbed the *T* off the sign! And she did it for the Titans—for me. I was forever hers. That's why seeing her on the memorial bench out front at 2:20 every afternoon is the highlight of my day, even if she doesn't see me back.

I wonder if Mitzy sits on the bench at 7:20 every morning too. I wouldn't know because I come in through the back in the morning, so I can take a loop around the track. Not running or jogging. I walk it slow, listening to the quiet, letting my creative juices flow, waiting for story ideas to pop up.

I guess I forgot to mention—I write stories. No big deal or anything, it's just my outlet, my escape. I make up people, give them problems, and let them play things out. Walking the track as the sun comes up, tuning my brainwaves to my stride, to my breath, maybe to the universe, that's when inspiration sometimes strikes. Anyway, I never pass the memorial bench on the way into school, so if she's there, I miss my chance. Which is probably just as well, because there's only so much rejection a guy can take.

So here I am today, on my way home. Amity Street dumps me into our little downtown, two streets over from where I live. If today were any other day, I'd walk straight under the "Fort Pippin Welcomes You" banner, pass the stretch of shops and tea spots, turn right at the indie bookstore, walk another quarter mile, and let the little saltbox of monotony at 25 Prospect welcome me home.

But as it turns out, this isn't any other day. For some reason, instead of walking right past the former post office building, I stop and look up. First, to the ground-floor awning of Blue Marble Novelties, then to the Loose Goose Café on the second floor, and on to the darkened window on the top floor, which is where I see something I've never noticed before. It's a handwritten sign in the window that says, "Fortunes and Futures, $8—OPEN." Hmm. Maybe it's new, or maybe I just never looked up before. Not that it matters. It's just a piece of brown cardboard someone has taken a Sharpie to. It's nothing.

2

*Y*eah, I tell myself as I open the front door to the old post office building and head up the stairs, *it's nothing.* It's just me not feeling like going home yet. It's me wondering why eight dollars for your fortune? Why not five or ten, or why not split the difference and call it seven-fifty? It's me wanting a little distraction from my latest Mitzy Singer diss, that's all. I climb to the third floor.

Weird, the stairs don't end in a lobby or a landing. They end at a desk. A desk pushed so close to the staircase, I have to stop at the last step. It smells spicy up here, like cloves or maybe nutmeg. And it's as quiet as my social life. Maybe I should turn around and leave. I probably should. I have a ton of homework on my phone. Besides, I don't believe in psychics or clairvoyants or any of that stuff. Yeah, I probably should get out of here.

The only thing on the desk is a bell, the kind you have to pick up by the handle to ring, so I do, just to hear how it sounds. Funny, it barely whispers, as if it resents being disturbed. I set it down and lean against the railing, waiting for nothing to happen. I'm going to give this to the count of thirty, then I'm out of here. This was a stupid idea to begin with.

One, two, three...seventeen, eighteen, nineteen...

I don't see or hear her coming. She's just there, her short silver hair dipping over her sea-gray eyes. She's wearing a flowy green dress that ends just above her ankle bracelet, and she's barefoot. I've never seen her before, and I'm Fort Pippin born and raised.

"How good to see you." Her voice is throaty but soft. "I'm glad you decided to come." She says it like she knows me, which she doesn't. Or like she was expecting me, which she wasn't, since I didn't even know I was coming here myself.

"Um, hi." Suddenly I wish I'd only given her until fifteen.

She scans my face, then smiles a small smile. "It's okay to be nervous."

"I'm not nervous."

She nods. "Or to be unsure."

"I've never done this before, that's all."

"I know." Her smile grows a little bigger. "Come through then." She motions for me to skirt the desk and join her in the hallway.

"I'm Abe," I say, but maybe she already knows that too.

"Abe." She repeats my name slowly, like she's tasting it, seeing if it's done right, or if it needs a little salt. "Hello, Abe. My name is Zinnia, like the flower. Shall we get started?"

Her bare feet make little pings against the floor as she leads me to a door halfway down the hall. She pulls a skeleton key out of her dress pocket and slips it into the lock.

"Here we are then." She opens the door onto a small square room, darkened except for the cracks of sunlight that slip around the edges of the window blind. There's a card table and a few stools standing on the hardwood floor, and there's something hanging on one wall—a mirror maybe, or a painting, I'm not sure. The smell is stronger in here, the cloves, or maybe it's black licorice.

She lights on one of the stools. "You don't believe in this, do you?"

"In what?" I ask.

"This." She sweeps her arm around the room. "In me."

"I didn't say that."

"You didn't have to. Take a seat."

I take the stool opposite her and reach for my wallet. "Do I pay first?"

She sighs, as if earthly matters like money bore her. "Let's wait till the end. I only accept payment if the visitor gets what he came for."

"But I didn't come for anything."

"We'll see about that."

Now that my eyes are adjusting to the dark, I notice a deck of cards on the table. Zinnia picks up the top card and lays it face up on the table. It's a white crescent moon in a black sky. Something is sitting on the hook of the moon. It's hard to tell—the card is upside down to me—but I think it's a cat, a black-and-white cat dangling its legs into outer space. Zinnia touches the image, her finger tracing the curve of the moon.

"What does it mean?" I ask.

She admires the card a moment longer, then pins her eyes on mine. "What is making you unhappy, Abe?"

"When did I say I was unhappy?"

One corner of her mouth turns up. "No one comes to me unless they're unhappy about something. Missing something. Needing something."

I feel sweat collecting on the back of my neck. The spicy scent is even sharper now, almost peppery. I really should leave, go home, start my homework.

"All right." She crosses her legs. "It's all right. Let's just continue, shall we?"

She turns over another card. It's a gemstone, cobalt blue against a neon yellow background. Zinnia looks surprised this time, maybe even a little startled. "Wow," she says, rubbing her chin. Then she just sits there, staring at the card, at me, at the card again.

"Everything okay?" I ask.

"Mmm," she murmurs, which is pretty vague if you ask me. "Everything is…very interesting. You are an interesting fellow, Abe."

I almost laugh at this.

"Interesting isn't the first word most people would use to describe me."

She shoves the cards aside and drops her elbows onto the table. "You, Abe, are a sapphire moon. Highly unusual."

"Unusual. Now that's more like it."

"Let me ask you this." She uncrosses her legs. "If you could change something in your life right now, this very instant, what would it be?" Her gray eyes are bright somehow in the dim light of the room. She's looking through me, but not in the way Mitzy does. She's seeing into me.

I don't know what to say, so I say nothing.

"Maybe I can put it another way. If you could wish for something, what would it be?" She's leaning closer now.

"Okay, fine. If I could change something, I'd, you know—" And then I draw a blank.

"Actually, I don't think I do know."

I shift my weight on the stool. "I guess I'd be a different person. A person with a little more going on in their life. A few chocolate jimmies on my vanilla ice cream, y'know?"

Zinnia glances down at the cards.

"So anyway." I scratch my elbow, then my forehead. "What does it mean, the moon and the sapphire?"

"Well." She draws the word out to about five syllables. "There's good news and there's bad news. Which do you want first?"

"The bad."

"All right." She sucks in a breath. "Someone is going to die."

Okay, now she has crossed the line from nutty fortune teller to creepy person. "Um, you know what?" I push my stool back with a squeal. "I really have to be go—"

"The good news," she quickly adds, "is that you might be able to prevent it."

"Me? Who is it then—who's going to die?" I ask, which is stupid because I know none of this could possibly be true.

"I'm sorry. I'm afraid I don't know who it is. That's part of your challenge."

Yup, of *course* she doesn't know. Because she's a big fake. "No thanks, Zinnia. Challenge not accepted."

"But I thought you wanted some chocolate jimmies."

"Yeah, but this isn't what I meant." I stand up. "Or what I wanted."

"I don't pick out your cards, Abe," she tells me. "I only read them."

"Right." I reach for my wallet again.

She holds up her hands. "You don't owe me a penny. I'm just sorry you didn't get what you desired."

"O…kay, well, thanks for, yeah, thanks." I step to the door.

Something funny happens as I turn the knob, though. Well, not so much funny as bizarre. First, the door feels heavy. Then the scent in the room, the cloves and the licorice, grows fiery enough to knock me over.

"Abe?" I hear Zinnia say, but she sounds far away.

I look back to the room, but I don't see her.

"Abe!" she calls from whatever distant place she has run off to.

I pull open the door, but it's too heavy to hold on to. I'm heavy too. Heavy and off. Way, way off. A high-pitched wail is throbbing in the room. No, not in the room—in my head. Everything is vibrating. The darkness itself is vibrating, except that now it's not dark. There are colors and smells, textures and heat, prickles and tingles. And then it's all dark again.

3

Uff." I jolt when the pony cart jerks to a stop, shoving me against the driver's arm.

Something is wrong, very, very wrong.

It's jet black out except for a thin thread of moonlight, and I have no idea where I am. No idea how it got to be night either, or why I'm suddenly wearing boots and a cap. I pull myself up on the narrow bench, my heart careening in my chest.

"Sorry, Mr. Diemschutz," I croak. And I have no idea how I know this man's name.

My bones tell me it's been a long day, even though I don't know how I spent it. Working, I think. Selling something, maybe. Jewelry? Yes, jewelry, and this man is my boss. Wait, wait, wait. I don't have a job. And where did my sneakers go?

Obviously, this is a dream. Something in Zinnia's shop must have put me into a deep sleep. Maybe that clove-lic-orice scent I'd been breathing, that smell that got stronger and stronger the longer I stayed? I must be curled up on her floor right now, or parked on her stool with my face planted on the card table. This must be what they call a lucid dream, where you know you're dreaming even while it's happening. Hopefully, I'll wake up soon, but in the meantime, I guess I'll just go along for the ride. What else can I do?

The pony draws back again and gives a startled snort.

"Shall I see what's the matter with Polly?" I ask. I have never said *shall* in my entire life. And why do I have an English accent?

"No need," Mr. Diemschutz answers. "This is my gate."

In the faint moonlight, I can just make out the sign on the gate: Workman's Club. Suddenly I remember—no, that's not right. I can't be remembering this stuff, because I didn't know it before. But in this dream, this incredibly vivid dream, I know my boss lives at this social club. He manages the place, and the jewelry business is a side act. Wow, not just a vivid dream, but a detailed one too.

"Go on now." Mr. Diemschutz takes off his hat, revealing a crop of curly black hair and a steep forehead. "Your mum will be fretting."

"My…mum?"

"Doubt she'll get a wink till she hears the bolt turn behind you." He runs his hand along the length of his pony stick. "Cannot say I blame her. No one belongs on these Whitechapel streets after dark."

Whitechapel. I know that name from somewhere. Something about Victorian England, about London, about the slums. I look up at this guy's top hat and down at his wheels. He doesn't belong in my century. He belongs in the 1800s. This is the weirdest dream ever.

I jump down from the cart and button my vest against the windy night. I have never owned a vest. I have never worn wooden buttons. I have never stood on a cobblestone street before. How did these things get into my dream? "See you on Monday, sir."

"Good night, Asher."

So my name is Asher here. Noted. Anyway, I may not know exactly how to get so-called home to my so-called mum, but my feet seem to have an idea, so I tag along. I cross the fog-wrapped street, my boot heels clicking against the cobblestones. As I go, though, something makes me take a backward glance. My boss is standing inside the wrought-iron gate now, lighting a match and peering down, as if he's trying to get a better look at something on the ground. He makes a hoarse sound, like a muffled cry, and then he drops the match and runs into the clubhouse, the heavy door slamming shut behind him.

My palms get sweaty and my breath quickens, as if something bad is truly happening. Weird. I thought the beauty of a lucid dream was that you don't have to be afraid, because you know it's not really happening. So why does this feel so bizarrely realistic? "Pull yourself together," I whisper to myself, then head back toward the gate to see what spooked Mr. Diemschutz.

"Uff," I grunt for the second time in five minutes.

Halfway across the street I collide with someone running in the opposite direction. Someone wearing a coarse, oversized coat and smelling like a pub. In the mist I can't make out his face, but I hear panting, heavy and fast.

"Sorry, I didn't see—" I begin.

The stranger puts two large hands on my shoulders and pushes me away. The hands, sharp and bony, pack so much force that I lose my balance, stumbling backward, almost falling over. By the time I right myself, the stranger is sprinting down the street, the blackness swallowing him up in an instant.

Polly picks this moment to stamp her hooves, which is probably horse-speak for "Hello? Guarding the jewelry cart alone here." Why would Mr. Diemschutz do that—why would he leave his pony and his wares alone in the middle of the slums in the middle of the night?

"Don't worry, girl," I say to Polly. "I'm sure master will be back in a trice." Whatever *trice* means.

Part of me still wants to see what my boss was looking at on the ground, what scared him, see if he needs any help, but I shrug it off. Dreams are always full of weird incidents, right? So instead of investigating, I head to my dream home, where I hope things are a little less intense.

Home turns out to be a three-story tenement that looks like the set for a horror flick. It's dark, sunken, decrepit. Did I mention dark? Once inside, I feel my way up the rickety stairs, listening to the pitter-patter of rodent feet along the steps, silently cursing Zinnia and her sleep-inducing spices.

On the second-floor landing, my feet take me to a door at the end of a narrow hallway. I pull a key out of my pocket, slip it into the door lock, and step inside. Even though it's pitch black, I can feel how cramped the space is. The air is damp and still, and it smells fishy and vinegary, like when my grandma gets on one of her salted-herring-and-pickled-cucumber benders. I close the door and feel for the bolt.

"Asher, is that you?" A woman in a flannel nightgown appears, carrying a candle lamp.

Now I can see that I'm in a small room that's a kitchen, bedroom, and sitting room rolled into one. The low, sooty ceiling reflects the light from her candle. Bloomers and undershirts hang to dry on a cord that sags across the length of the room. It's hot in here, as if the place thinks it's still summer.

The woman—my mum?—is standing in the doorway of the flat's only other room, a closet-sized space she probably sleeps in. She hasn't been asleep, though. She's been waiting up. I bend down to untie my boots. "Safe and sound."

"You must be hungry." She flips her dark braid over her shoulder. "I'll fix you a plate."

I don't look her in the face. I don't care what she looks like. She's just my dream mother, after all. She'll disappear as soon as this snooze ends. "Too tired," I tell her. "I'll have it in the morning."

I go to the low, flimsy bed in the corner and flop onto my back. The way I figure it, the sooner I go to sleep, the sooner I can wake up, and when I do, I'll be where I belong. In the twenty-first century. In the little saltbox of monotony that's my real home. That's how it has always worked for me—if I wake up within a dream, I wake up for real. I can't wait.

"You'd better give me your shirt in the morning." She shakes her head. "How did you manage to get it so dirty? You were selling jewelry, not coal."

I can feel the stranger's hands on my shoulders again, hard, pointy, powerful. "Sorry. 'Night." Then I roll onto my side and wait for morning, for Fort Pippin, for this insanely lifelike REM cycle to end.

4

I hear my "mum" drag herself out of bed while it's still dark out. Once she lights a candle, I can see her in her room, pulling on black stockings and boots, throwing a coat over her nightgown, grabbing her water basin. I pretend to be asleep as she walks past me on her way out the door. A minute later I hear an outdoor water pump squealing. When she comes back inside, she puts the tea kettle on and goes to her room.

And then it hits me.

It's morning, and I'm still in the wrong place and the wrong time. Which means...I don't think this is a dream after all. I think this is really happening. A scream rises up in my chest, and it's all I can do to shove it back down before it reaches my throat. No wonder everything feels so authentic here. No wonder I can't will myself to fly or breathe under water or any of those fantastic things they say you can script out in a lucid dream. This is all for real.

My heart hammers in my chest, and it's a good thing I'm lying down because I'm so dizzy I can't budge. I'm really in nineteenth-century Whitechapel. I can't believe it, much less understand it.

Even if I don't know how it happened, I do know it's all Zinnia's fault. Zinnia and her sapphire moon, her big changes, her chocolate jimmies. She probably expects me to save someone's life while I'm here too. Ha! Sorry, Zinnia, I won't have time for any of that. I'll be putting every shred of energy into getting myself out of here. Period.

Unless...

Ugh, what if I can't escape until I fulfill her prediction? What if I can't go home until I prevent someone from dying?

The teapot whistles, jarring me fully awake. I get up and walk across the cold floor to take the pot off the stove.

"Did I wake you?" Mum asks when she emerges from her room, her hair up in a bun, her skirt and shawl on. She talks partly in English, partly in Yiddish.

"I-I thought I'd walk you to work," I say, even though I don't know where that is. I've got to keep myself moving or my head is going to explode. It might as well be a slog through the city.

"Don't be silly. I walk myself to work every day. This is your one day to sleep in."

"Too late for that." I feel protective of her somehow, this woman who's a stranger but who's also my mother here. I want to see what kind of sweatshop she toils in, and how far she has to trudge to get there. I'm actually relieved that I don't already know—it means I'm still Abe, or at least I'm not completely Asher. Yet.

"That's sweet of you, hon, but—"

"Did you say there's some supper left?"

"Herring, on the shelf." She pours two cups of tea. "Give it a smell, make sure it's still good. There's pumpernickel in the breadbox."

So no refrigerator, no indoor plumbing, no heat. This is going to be a long day. I grab a chunk of brown bread and call it a meal.

It's still twilight when we head out, the damp air reeking of horse droppings and trash. The fog hangs in the doorways and alleys like ghosts. Overhead, bickering voices spill out of an open window. I think of that old Animals song I hear sometimes in the car—something about a dirty city and the sun withholding its shine.

"You really don't have to do this, Ash." Mum pulls her woolen shawl tighter around her shoulders. "You should be doing whatever you want on your Sunday off."

I finally allow myself now what I refused to do last

night—I take a good look at her face. Her harsh existence has dug lines around her mouth and drawn circles under her eyes, but she's still pretty, with hazel eyes, tawny skin, and a way of talking that shows off her teeth.

"I *am* doing what I want," I tell her. "And I have the rest of the day to laze about." *Laze about*—did I really say that? It's like this place, this time, is drawing me in, taking me over.

We cross over a road marked Bloomsbury Street and head east, then walk in silence. Mum keeps her head down, probably trying to avoid horse pies, while I watch the city yawn itself awake. Foot traffic picks up as men plod to work, probably to the river docks. Every once in a while, a horse trods by with a cartful of wares. Above it all, the gulls screech in loud, urgent squawks, as if they're singing along to that same oldie—about needing to get out of here or die trying. I swallow down my panic.

"What will you do with yourself today?" Mum asks. We're passing by a place called Mitre Square, where hawkers are setting up their market stalls.

"Um…" Crap, what would Asher do on his day off? What *could* he do around here? "I suppose I'll, y'know…"

"More hanging around the stables?"

"Maybe." Apparently, Asher likes horses.

Mum steps over some broken glass. "How I would love to send you to the Veterinary College one day." So Asher wants to be a vet. Yeah, that seems right. He wants to do dissections and study anatomy and stuff. A real animal lover. "You know that, don't you, Asher? That I would if I could."

"I don't want to go to Veterinary College, Mum," I tell her. "I just like hanging about the horses sometimes, that's all." *Hanging about?*

She offers me an apologetic smile. "Sweet of you to say, anyway. You are a good boy."

We walk on, along proper English-sounding roads like Aldgate and Whitechapel High Street, passing the Petticoat

Lane Marketplace and sidestepping trash. It's a regular morning on a regular street, I guess—and a long walk for a job that probably pays peanuts. She will never, ever be able to send her son to college. She'll always be dirt poor, just like she is now. That's the rotten truth. And the reason I care about her is that this is real. I really am her son, at least in this crazy version of the world.

"Mrs. Bidwell took in a street cat, did I tell you?" Mum asks.

"I don't think so."

"It has no tail, but it has extra toes, that's what she says."

"Huh." Mrs. Bidwell must live in the building. Well, if her new pet is any kind of mouser, I hope she lets it loose on the staircase.

"She says she'll pay you to feed it when she goes to visit her sister, how's that?"

I'm about to answer, but something distracts me. What's this? Just ahead, by that brick wall fronting a row of buildings. There are two cops standing there, and another man, and they're looking at something on the wall. At handwriting. Mum, with her head still down, doesn't notice, but I do. The chalk graffiti says:

The Juwes are
The men that
Will not be blamed
For nothing

The Juwes? Is that supposed to say…Jews? And what does that mean, *will not be blamed for nothing?* I want to get within earshot of the cops, but I don't want to worry Mum. If I could think straight, if I were in the right place and time, I might be able to break it down, but I can't.

"Did you hear what I said?" Mum asks.

"Hmm? Oh, right." I force my eyes off the graffiti. I'll just have to wait until my return trip to check it out. "Yes, I'll feed the cat."

"Good. I already let her know you would." She checks her hair bun. "For free."

Yup, that sounds about right.

We leave the chalk graffiti behind and walk past a church bell workshop, a shuttered-up mill, a railway station. Finally, Mum stops in front of the Bryant & May Matchstick Company. It's a mammoth building with women and girls pouring in and out, the sharp tang of phosphorus piercing the air. Mum is just another one of those women, just another matchstick girl, another brick in the wall.

"Thank you for the lovely company." She offers me a tired smile. "I'll see you tonight."

"Tonight?" It's barely morning now. How long is her shift, anyway?

She kisses me on the cheek. "Around seven, I expect. Oh, bring Mr. Kraskov our copy of *Di Nayes*, would you? I forgot to bring it by yesterday."

Di Nayes means *The News* in Yiddish. It must be a local paper. "Mr. Kraskov?"

"Our upstairs neighbor. I've told you about him." She pulls my vest closed. "The butcher, remember? Number 38."

"Oh, right."

"Go on now, go have yourself a day off."

I give her arm a squeeze. "See you later."

As I walk away, I can feel her eyes on me, watching me as far as she can. Right before I take the first turn in the road, I wave, and she raises her hand to me, and then we turn in our opposite directions—she to make matchsticks, me to do I don't know what. Clearly, we're both going to have a long, rotten day.

I pick up my pace now, passing a corner bookshop, a church, and a place called a "haberdasher"—men's clothes by the looks of it. And now I see the brick wall again. This time, I want to eavesdrop on the cops, or at least get a closer look at the graffiti.

Wait, where is it? Where's *The Juwes are the men who will not be blamed for nothing*? I could swear it was right here on this stretch of wall, but there's no sign of it now. I step closer. Nothing but dusty bricks. I look up and down the street for the cops, but there are no uniforms, just tradesmen and marketers.

Maybe I'm on the wrong street. Maybe I'm just tired. Or maybe Zinnia sent me to a place that isn't even internally consistent. Yeah, thanks a load, Zinnia.

"Coming through, coming through!" shouts a voice from behind.

It's a man barreling down the road on a bike, the old-fashioned kind with the jumbo front wheel. He's huffing and puffing and red in the face, like he's late for a wedding or something. I step aside to let him pass, then turn my gaze back to the wall. The graffiti is still gone. Or maybe it was never here, I don't know. I don't know anything anymore, including and especially how to get out of here. I shove my fists into my pockets and schlep the rest of the way back to the tenement.

The flat smells a little like my school locker, stuffy and stale, so I open the small window over my bed and lie down, thinking I might actually fall back to sleep—anything to avoid thinking about what's happening to me. No such luck, though. I'm wide awake, as if I'd just chugged a couple of cans of Red Bull. Wide awake but with no ideas. No idea how Zinnia got me here, no idea how to save someone from dying, no ideas whatsoever.

The window above me lets in the din of the street—peddlers shouting out their wares, cart wheels creaking against cobblestone, kids laughing, mothers scolding. After a while I notice another, closer noise. It's a scraping sound, like wood against wood, as if someone upstairs is struggling to open their window.

Then I hear a voice, drifting in from directly above. A girl's voice. "Finally," she says, her voice muffled by the breeze. "Fresh air at last."

I sit up. Blink. Rub my eyes. Could it be?

"Beam me up, Scotty," the voice pleads. Then softer, sadder, with an edge of desperation. "Please, just beam me up."

I want to laugh. I want to cry. I want to jump up and down. I get on my knees, eye level to the window. "Mitzy?"

Silence.

"Mitzy, is that you?" *Please, please let me not be hallucinating.*

"I—I know you." She hesitates. "Who—?"

"It's me," I practically shout. "Abe Pearlman."

"Abe? Abe! Where are you? What happened to us?"

"I don't know." I crane my head, squinting up through the laundry lines cluttered with petticoats and bedsheets. I still can't see her. "I mean, I sort of know. I went to this, this fortune teller, and she told me—"

"What a freak."

"What?"

"Not you," she says. "Her. Zinnia."

"Wait, you know her?"

"As of yesterday I do," she tells me. "I went to, y'know, have her look into her crystal ball and tell me everything's going to be okay. Instead I got this. I got the worst."

"It's not the worst." Which might be the stupidest thing I've ever said.

"You don't know the half of it, Abe. Just you wait and see."

"I'll be right up." I jump out of the bed. "What apartment are you in?"

"No idea."

"No problem." I stick my feet into my boots. "You're directly over my apartment, right? I can figure it out. Do you know the name?"

"Um, wait, I got this." She makes a low hum. "It's Krakov—no, Kraskov."

"Kraskov, perfect." I grab the copy of *Di Nayes* off the kitchen table and head out the door, wondering if I'm a bad person because I'm glad Mitzy is here with me, glad she's stuck in this time warp, this tenement, this disaster.

Climbing the dingy stairs to the top floor, my mind strays back to last school year, around Halloween time. Mitzy wasn't in class one day. Or the next day. Or the rest of that week. I heard she was on a leave of absence, unexplained. It didn't take long for the rumor mill to start filling in the blanks. She ran away, she got thrown into juvie, stuff like that. Yup, everyone always figured Mitzy was Trouble, or at least Troubled, just because she's the kind of person who keeps to herself. I was waiting for them to say she robbed a bank or joined the circus, but then one day she was back. She looked the same as ever, except her hair was blue. It's been blue ever since.

I never heard the real reason she was out of school, and I didn't really care, as long as she was back. But now I have to wonder if she was on one of these space-time trips. Like, maybe this isn't her first time through the wormhole. Not that it matters. Well, maybe it does, but I don't have time to work that out right now.

One flight up, I knock on the door with the mezuzah. It feels like an hour until she answers it. I can't wait to see someone from the twenty-first century, someone who can tell me I haven't gone crazy, that I'm not alone in it. But most of all, I can't wait to see *her*, to see Mitzy. As the door finally starts to open, I break into my first smile since I blew into this joint.

But it's not Mitzy. It's a man. Short, stocky, dark eyes, balding. And most definitely not smiling.

"Mr. Kraskov?" I guess.

"*Ver zayt ir?*" he asks in Yiddish—who are you?

I hand him the newspaper. "*Nat aykh*—here you go. From my mother." I don't know how I pull that line out. I'm used to listening to my grandma talk in Yiddish, but I hardly ever speak it. It's this place, this time, sucking me in.

He's already shutting the door in my face when a voice from inside calls, "Duvid, *ver iz do*—who's there?" A small brown-haired woman appears in the doorway, wiping her hands on her apron. She looks around the same age as my mother—I mean, my here-mother, my mum. She's younger than my real mother, my there-mother.

"Good morning," I say. "I mean, *gut-morgn*."

"It is all right," the woman says with a Russian accent. "I have English, some. I am Bina Kraskov. And you, you are?"

"Abe—I mean, Asher, ma'am."

Mr. Kraskov plants a scowl on me while he talks to the woman in Yiddish. "This boy, his mother usually brings me the paper. Not him."

"I am pleased to meet you," she says. "You will come in please, yes?"

Mr. Kraskov groans at this, but he steps aside to let me into his hovel. A pot is boiling on the coal stove, and the room smells like meat, like maybe calf's liver. Otherwise, it's exactly like my flat.

Bina Kraskov smooths her apron. "I move in with Duvid few days ago. He is my—how you say—he is *mishpuchah*. He is my, I am his—oy."

A voice calls in from the back room, "He's Mama's brother-in-law." Not just any voice. Mitzy's. "And he's my uncle." Then she's in the room with us.

5

It's Mitzy, all right, but it's not Mitzy. The black jeans are gone, and so are the spiked blue hair, the wrist bangles, and the ear studs. This Mitzy—the new Mitzy, or maybe it's the old Mitzy—is scrubbed clean, wearing a simple dress, her chocolate hair hanging down to her shoulders. She's still looking through me, but in a different way somehow.

"Hello, I'm Maya," she says.

I'm about to introduce myself, but suddenly the air stops in my lungs. That look in Mitzy's eyes. She's not looking through me. It's something else. Something worse.

"I'm blind," she says.

I open my mouth, but no words come out. As if there are words for this.

She holds out her arm in my general direction. I step forward and take her hand in mine. She pulls me a little closer and whispers, "Help me."

I nod, and then I realize she can't see me nodding. "I will," I whisper back.

Mr. Kraskov harrumphs his disapproval—disapproval of what, I don't know. Of me? Of me talking to Mitzy? Of whispering? Mitzy's here-mother must notice his glare too, because she says in Yiddish, "Duvid, you don't want to be late for your first English lesson, do you?"

He narrows his eyes at me and throws about a thousand silent darts. I half expect him to grab me by the collar and drag me out, but he doesn't. He just turns and walks out of the apartment.

When the door closes behind him, Mrs. Kraskov switches back to English. "Mr. Kraskov is start English class at Workman's Club."

"I...yes, great." I scratch the back of my neck. "That's really great."

"You like cup tea?"

Mitzy answers for me. "We'd like to go out."

"Out?" her mother asks.

"For a walk. Please, Mama, I need air."

Mrs. Kraskov folds her arms and says nothing.

Mitzy tries again. "It's fine, Mama. Abe—I mean, Ash, Asher—is a family friend of Uncle Duvid." Which almost makes me laugh, because Duvid Kraskov doesn't seem like the kind of guy who has friends.

"I..." Mrs. Kraskov presses her lips together, poised for a no.

"We won't be gone long." Mitzy pulls my arm toward the door.

"Be back before your uncle," her mother warns.

"Yes, Mama. Just a turn or two around the block."

As soon as we step into the hallway, Mitzy takes in a mouthful of air and busts a gut. "No, no, no!" she rails. "What is this? The slum. The time warp. And like that's not bad enough, Zinnia had to make me blind to boot!"

I lead her down the hallway to the rickety staircase, wondering how we're going to get her safely down.

"We've got to get out of here, Abe." The misery in her voice is like its own language. "Now."

"I know." I just don't know how. All I know is that this isn't a dream, and we're not simply going to wake up from it.

"What did you wish for?" she asks. "From Zinnia?"

"To be a different person," I confess. "How about you?"

"I said I wouldn't mind it if I never had to lay eyes on an algebra equation again. My eyes, ha."

"She's evil."

"Evil? That's not the word I'd use," she says. "But if you insist on being proper, then fine, evil."

I go down the first step and turn around to face her. "Give me your hands."

She frowns.

"Don't worry. I'm just going to help you down the stairs, not dance you to midnight."

"Fine." She puts her hands out, and I take them. I don't tell her about the mice scurrying along the steps. She doesn't need to know that. We take the first step, then another, and it does sort of feel like a dance. To me, anyway.

We take the last few stairs, and I push open the door to the outside. It's warmer out now, so I unbutton my vest. Mitzy's nostrils quiver as she takes in a breath of the outdoors—the trash, the dung, the sweat. The street teems with women in long dresses, boys in short pants, a few men in top hats, everything about them looking rumpled and worn. No one smiles. No one has a reason to.

"So what happened with you and Zinnia?" I loop my arm through hers to guide her. "Did she read your cards?"

"Yup. I got the wind and water." She takes an uncertain step, and we start to stroll.

"What did she say it means?"

"I..." She rubs her forehead. "Ugh, it makes me sick to think about it."

"That bad?"

"For me it is. What did you get?"

"The moon and a sapphire. She said someone's going to die unless I prevent it."

Mitzy winces. "Who? Who's going to die?"

"No clue. And I have the feeling I'm going to be stuck in Victorian England until I figure it out."

I try to focus on steering Mitzy clear of the people and the garbage, but my head is swirling. Those women sitting in the doorways, is one of them in danger? What about that man pushing the wobbly cart? Overhead, what looks like a broken coat rack hangs halfway out a window, and I worry it's going to fall on some little boy. There are so many people crammed into this street, and any one of them could be at risk. Any one of them, or none of them.

"Weird," Mitzy says after a while. "My fortune, it wasn't anything like yours. She just said I'm going on a long boat ride. Across the sea."

"But...what's so horrible about that?"

"If you must know, I can't look at a boat without barfing. Violently."

"Oh."

"You better not be laughing, Abe Pearlman."

"I'm not." A hungry-looking dog starts tagging alongside us, wagging its grimy tail. "It's just, a boat ride seems like a pretty small price to pay to get out of here. At least no one's going to die on your watch."

"Yeah, except I don't know how long I'll have to wait around for it. I mean, I could picture it if we were rich. But we're poor, Abe, dirt poor. People like us don't go on cruises, you know?"

The mutt lets out a single bark and trots away. "All right, so we'll hang around the docks sometime, stow away, travel the world."

"*We'll* stow away? Abe, you have to be here to save a life, remember?"

"Yeah, but...okay, I'll save a life and *then* we'll stow away."

"Well, the way my mother and uncle hover, I don't see how I'll ever get close to any ships. I don't even know where they dock or how to get there. Or where they sail to. Or anything."

"All right," I say, "so we'll have to—"

"Let's talk about something else. Tell me about the new you. Do you know what your story here is?"

I step over a scat pile. "Me? I have a single mom who works at a matchstick factory, and I'm apprenticing with a jewelry merchant. I think I once did a stint as a chimney sweep."

"Sounds like we both won the crap lottery," she sighs. "From what I gather, I started going blind when I was little. My father died last month, so that's why we moved in with his brother, this Duvid guy. What a surly-boots."

I laugh out loud.

"What?" she demands.

"You just called your uncle a surly-boots."

"I did not. I called him a grouch. Whatever. I'm just glad he's out working six days a week."

I skirt her around a clump of boys fighting over a loaf of round bread. "What does he do, your uncle?"

"He's a kosher butcher at some slaughterhouse."

"And he doesn't speak any English," I say.

"None."

"Then how do you understand what he's saying?"

"Don't know," she says. "I mean, I always knew a few words, but now—it's like someone planted a Yiddish language chip in my head. Freaky."

"No kidding." I watch a couple of pigeons fighting over a crumb of bread in the street. "Hey, how do you think the real Maya and Asher are handling twenty-first century Fort Pippin?"

"What?" She halts. "Did that really happen? Is that how this works?"

"Dunno, but they had to go somewhere, didn't they? I just hope Asher isn't flunking my math quiz as we speak."

Mitzy starts walking again. "Maya better not be talking up...anyone. I have a rep to uphold."

I can't think of anything to say after that. We have one of those gawky silences until she says, "Tell me what's out here."

I look around at the dirt and the gloom. "Well, to our left we have the castle of the grand duchess. On our right, you'll find a splendid five-star restaurant. And straight ahead is the finest dressmaker in all of London."

I turn to see if she likes my joke. Nope, not even the hint of a smile.

When I look forward again, I find a grim sight—Duvid Kraskov walking in our direction. I don't understand—he's been out for barely ten minutes. What happened to his English lesson? Did he get kicked out for bad behavior? I hold Mitzy's arm tighter and stop walking, scanning the street for a way out.

"Abe?" Mitzy knows something is wrong.

"Let's just duck into—no, too late."

"Too late for what? What's happening?"

"It's your uncle, heading our way. He sees us."

Her arm stiffens.

Now Mr. Kraskov's brusque voice rises over the congestion. "Maya, that is you?" he calls. Then he's standing right in front of us.

"Uncle Duvid, what about your lessons?" she asks in Yiddish.

He rubs his chin and looks back over his shoulder. "They have the Workman's Club sealed off. There was a murder in the yard there last night."

"A murder!" Mitzy pulls me a little closer.

A murder in the club yard. The Workman's Club. Where my boss lives. Suddenly everything I was trying to forget about last night floods in. The pony flinching. Mr. Diemschutz jumping down to investigate. The stranger pushing me aside on the street. *A murder.*

"What happened—who was killed?" Mitzy asks her uncle.

He shrugs. "A woman. They say it's the Ripper's work."

The Ripper. All at once, I feel a hunk of ice whack my chest and shatter into a thousand shards. Mitzy and I, we've been plunked down in the middle of the Jack the Ripper murders. And my boss and I, we must have interrupted the fiend in the act last night! We were actually there, right there where it happened, while it was happening.

Oh, crap. Could I have prevented it if I'd shown up a minute earlier? Am I too late already?

"This is no time to be out on the streets," Mr. Kraskov tells Mitzy. "Come with me. Home, where you belong."

"But Uncle, we won't go far."

"You are not to be out, and you are not to be with any no-goodnik boys."

No-goodnik boys. Does he think all boys are no-good-niks, or just me?

"Asher and I are just—" Mitzy tries again.

But Duvid Kraskov already has his hand on her arm. He is her uncle in this world, her guardian, her controller. Mitzy lets go of me, mouthing *Later.*

Later? I can't wait until later. I want to tell her right this very minute that, I don't know, that I'm here for her. That I hope she has a bed to sleep in. That we'll figure a way out. But there's nothing I can do right now, nothing but stoke my hate. I hate Mr. Kraskov for stealing Mitzy away. I hate Zinnia for banishing us here. And I hate myself for being the helpless clod that I am. A helpless clod, alone on a street where Jack the Ripper has left his mark.

I don't know what to do with myself, so I start walking in the direction of the Workman's Club. The closer I get, the more people fill the street, until half of London seems to be crowded around the gate. Everyone jockeys for a view of the yard, straining for a glimpse of the crime scene. Men, women, even little kids press in, chattering away, spirits high, like they're in line for a carnival.

"I want to see!" bellows one little boy, jumping and squirming, as if he expects to find elephants and clowns if he can just stop for a peek. His mother pulls him away. "I want to see!" he moans and pulls.

"Uff." I take it in the gut when a rumpled woman, busy fussing with her pipe, walks straight into me.

"Have ye a light, lad?" she winks up at me.

"I'm sorry, no."

"Bah, 'tis that kind of day. No matches. No hotcakes. And another day's pay lost." She nods in the direction of the clubhouse. "I'm their charwoman, don't you know. Can't get near the place today."

"Wait, you work for Mr. Diemschutz?" I ask her.

"His wife, really." She pushes her bonnet farther back on her head. "So busy she is, running all them festivities and such for the foreign folks. Half of 'em don't speak a word of English, mind you. Most of 'em don't have two shillings to rub together."

I look to the clubhouse, closed up tight.

"Now this." She tsk-tsks with a click of her tongue. "And to think the fiend struck again an hour later."

"I'm sorry, what?" The ice shards on my chest are piercing my skin now.

"Haven't ye heard?" The woman tucks her pipe into her skirt and crosses her arms. "Over on Mitre Square…are ye all right now, lad? You look a little peaked around the gills."

If I'd only grabbed that stranger on the street last night, I could have prevented the murder on Mitre Square. I could have fulfilled Zinnia's prophecy. Maybe I really am stuck here forever. Maybe I'm doomed to spend the rest of my life peddling jewelry and dodging rodents.

The old woman narrows her eyes at me. "Ye should take yourself away from here, boy. A drop of gin wouldn't do ye no harm, either."

My throat starts to burn. I take a gulp of the morning air, but it doesn't help.

"Ye do have a place to go, don't ye?" she inquires. "Ye seem well enough looked after."

"Yes, ma'am."

"Good." She gives me a smile with more gaps than teeth. "I'm off to the Kings Stores Pub, meself. Top of the morning to ye."

Then she picks up her skirts and moves on.
Leaving me, once again, alone.

6

Yesterday ended up being the most agonizingly long day in the history of all days. Once Duvid Kraskov yanked Mitzy away, I had no one to talk to and nothing to do. It was just me, myself, and my thoughts—not a good combination. I spent the rest of the day in the flat, obsessing over our pathetic plight, over my missed opportunities. *Will there be another chance*, I kept asking myself, *another chance to save someone? Will Mitzy ever get a shot at boarding a boat?*

Then I started ruminating over what kind of chaos Asher and Maya might be creating for us. For all I know, that guy is failing me out of school, or daring to talk back when my sister calls him names. Mitzy's substitute could be mingling with the popular girls, raising her hand in class, doing all sorts of non-Mitzy stuff.

All day long I hoped Mitzy would call down to me through her window, but zilch. When my mum got home, long after dark, we ate days-old pickled herring and brown bread, and she told me all about the gossip buzzing around the factory. Gossip about the fiend, the Ripper. It was the worst day ever.

So when today dawns in a gray monotone, I'm actually glad to have somewhere to go, even if that somewhere is a job I know nothing about. I tear off another chunk of brown bread, lace up my boots, say goodbye to Mum, and head downstairs. Outside, the day matches my mood—overcast sky, gritty chimney smoke, sooty cobblestones. Perfectly miserable.

I pull up my jacket collar and keep my head down as I round the gate to the Workman's Club. Pushing open the clubhouse door, I find myself in a social hall set up with benches and a small stage at the front.

The room is empty. The building is silent.

"Hello?" I call. No response. "Mr. Diemschutz, sir?" I try again.

This time I hear sounds through the floorboards above, then a door opening, and finally feet on stairs. A woman appears at the far end of the room, her sandy hair in a single braid down her back, a coat thrown over her nightclothes, her feet in stockings. This must be Mrs. Diemschutz.

"Oh, Asher, it's you." Her hand goes to her chest as she walks over to me. "I thought perhaps…but no. Anyway, Mr. Diemschutz is at the inquest today. There was a terrible thing happened here Saturday night. You did hear about it?"

"Yes, ma'am."

"He'll be at the inquest all day. Possibly tomorrow too. I guess you have an unexpected holiday."

I nod, not knowing what to say. I want to say something comforting, but what?

She pushes some loose strands of hair off her forehead. "I'll let Mr. Diemschutz know we talked."

"Thank you. Oh, ma'am?"

"Yes?"

"Where is the inquest happening? If you don't mind my asking."

"The vestry hall on Cable Street." She digs her hands into her coat pockets. "But I wouldn't bother if I were you. The show is sure to be sold out."

"Right," I say, but she's already on her way back to the stairs.

Out on the street again, I wish I had Google Maps or even an old-fashioned paper map. It's okay, though, because the first person I ask knows how to direct me to Cable Street, and it's only a short walk. The vestry hall is a boxy, two-story stone building with a rounded front door. The problem, as Mrs. Diemschutz predicted, is that it's a packed house, and they aren't letting anyone else in. Instead, I join the loiterers huddled around the open window at the back of the building.

From inside, someone introduces himself as Coroner Wynne Baxter, presiding. After some talk I can't make out, I hear my boss's voice.

Mr. Diemschutz: "...I could not see what it was, so I sent my apprentice on his way, then jumped down from my barrow and struck a match. It was the figure of a woman."

Coroner: "What did you do next?"

Diemschutz: "I ran inside for a candle and went off at once to look for a police officer. The officer called in a doctor and an inspector, who questioned and searched everyone at the club."

Coroner: "Thank you, Mr. Diemschutz. That will be all for the moment, but please do not leave the premises. We shall take a twenty-minute recess."

Most of the loiterers drift away at this point. I keep my feet rooted to the spot, but my heart is racing away. Why did Zinnia send us back to this particular week? For me, it's to stop someone from dying, yes, but who? Assuming I haven't lost my chance already, that is.

Am I supposed to prevent the Ripper's next murder? Or am I supposed to shield the Ripper—like, keep him from getting caught? Or maybe it's not that direct. Maybe the Ripper is stalking a woman who has a little boy, a little boy who will die of neglect if he gets orphaned. Or maybe it has nothing to do with the Ripper at all. Let's face it, this future victim could be anyone. Maybe it's even Mitzy. Maybe she's the one I need to protect. But why would we have to travel to the Victorian slums for that? And how does her boat ride figure in? Ugh, I can't figure it out.

Suddenly something dawns on me. Mitzy said her uncle works six days a week. He had yesterday off, which means he's back to his butchering today. I run to Berner Street.

❧

Mitzy's mother answers the door. "Asher, everything is all

right? Why you are not working? Maya says you sell the jewels."

"Everything is fine, Mrs. Kraskov," I tell her. "Turns out I have the day off."

"What luck," Mitzy calls from inside the flat. "You're just in time to help shell."

"Shell?" I step in.

"Mama and I have taken up work." She sits at the kitchen table with a wooden bucket on her lap, a nutcracker in her hand, and an ocean of walnuts spread in front of her. "The costermonger on Sage Road is going to give us a shilling for every bucket we fill." Then under her breath she adds, "Whoopee."

I watch her feel along the table for a walnut, crack it, and pop the meat into the bucket. The shell goes into the washbasin at her feet. "We'll be rich by year's end, don't you expect, Mama?" You could cut her sarcasm with a butcher's knife.

Mrs. Kraskov sits down at the table and pulls a nutcracker out of her apron pocket. She starts shelling a walnut, but her eyes are on Mitzy's fingers.

"Here, let me," I tell Mitzy.

Mitzy shakes her head. "Take Mama's."

"No, you give, Maya," Mrs. Kraskov insists. "Asher and I, we work. If Asher does not mind."

"I'm fine, Mama." Mitzy stands firm. "Besides, don't you need to get to the market for Uncle's dinner? This is the perfect time."

Mrs. Kraskov looks to me. "I do not like for to leave Maya alone."

"I'm happy to help." I take the seat next to Mitzy and hold my hand out to Mrs. Kraskov.

She hesitates, then gives me the nutcracker and unties her apron. "I not be going long."

"I've got all day. Take your time."

"Thank you, Asher. Maya, you watch your fingers." She grabs her coat and basket from the door hook and heads out.

"What's going on with the walnuts?" I ask as soon as we're alone. "Trying to earn your way out from under the ogre?"

She rolls her eyes. "Mama told the ogre she wants to pitch in. Next thing you know, he makes a deal with the nut guy— the costermonger—and we're swimming in walnuts."

"Sheesh," I mutter to no one.

Mitzy cracks a few more nuts. "Mama should've gone to Annie's instead."

"Whose?"

"Annie. Our cousin in Brooklyn. That's where Mama should've taken us when Papa passed. Not here."

"Yeah, well." I tap the nutcracker against the table. "Our pal Zinnia seems to think we belong here in London."

"Freaking Zinnia."

"Yep." Then we just sit there.

"You want me to show you how?" Mitzy asks after a while.

"Hmm?"

"The nutcracker."

"Oh no, sorry. I was just busy, y'know, feeling wretched." I put a nut in the cracker and split the shell.

"At least we have snacks." She takes a nut from the bucket and slips it into her mouth. "You like these?"

"Walnuts? Don't know—I've only ever had them in brownies."

"Here then." She takes another nut from the bucket and moves closer. Touches my face, finds my mouth, and presses the nut to my lips.

Something in my belly wriggles and flutters.

When I was little, my mother—my real mother, my twenty-first-century mother, my then-and-there mother—used to tell me this one story at bedtime. She said that when sighted children close their eyes at night, blind children on the other side of the world get to borrow their vision. It was supposed to make me more willing to go to bed. It didn't. But now. Now if I could lend my sight to Mitzy, I'd close my eyes all day long.

I bite down on the nut.

"Good?" Her face is so close to mine, I can feel the tickle of her breath on my cheek. I nod. "Sort of buttery and smooth?" she asks softly, her voice more like air than sound.

"Mmm."

"Good," she says, but her tone changes. "Now, will you kindly tell me why you have the day off from work all of a sudden?" She sits back with a thump, a temper. "And stop keeping secrets from me, Abe Pearlman."

The nut turns dry and cold in my mouth. "No secrets, Mitzy, I swear. My boss had to be at the murder inquest today, that's all. He's the one who found the body."

"Oh. Sorry, I mean..." She lowers her head. "Look, you're my only source of info around here, and I can't stand the thought of you holding out on me."

"I'm not. I won't." Her hand is close enough for me to hold, but I don't because I'm that much of a loser. "I'd never do that."

"And I keep thinking, what if this is my life? Like this. Blind and cracking walnuts and sneaking around the ogre." She winds her hair around her finger. "What if we're doomed?"

"We're not."

"You're pretty good at that." She releases her hair.

"At what?"

She picks up another nut. "At sounding like you mean it, like you're positive, even though you don't have a clue."

"But..." She's right, of course. I don't have so much as an inkling.

The apartment door squeaks open then, and Mrs. Kraskov appears. "It is good going to market early morning. Much more fresher."

She comes to the table and takes four potatoes and an

onion out of her basket. "Here." She hands me the newspaper she was carrying under her arm. "You read us later, yes?"

"The news, sure."

"Not so much new." She winks. "It is from two days ago."

Two days seem so long ago already. Two days ago, I was living in the twenty-first century. I hadn't set foot in Zinnia's Fortunes and Futures, hadn't tripped down the rabbit hole of doom. Two days ago, the world still followed some basic rules, like time running forward.

I try to recall how it was, how it felt in that distant time. Yesterday at school, I had PE and we watched a video in Spanish class. But what did I have for lunch—the pizza or the veggie burger? Was I wearing my red hoodie or my Mets sweatshirt? Crap, I can't remember. It was so long ago. And so much has happened since then.

"First," Mrs. Kraskov says, "I have surprise." She reaches into her coat pocket and pulls out an envelope. "It is letter from cousin Annie in New York."

Mitzy lights up. "Read it to us."

Her mother sits down and tears open the letter. "'My dear Bina,'" she reads the Yiddish greetings. "'I hope you are settling smoothly into your new home. How is Maya adjusting?'"

Mrs. Kraskov reads on about cousin Annie's job sewing waistcoats, her husband's work as a bookbinder, and their twin daughters' antics. "'Now before I close,'" she continues, "'I will tell you something exciting I heard talk about. Something wonderf—'"

Mrs. Kraskov's voice trails off, her eyes scanning the lines at the end of the letter. Quickly, she folds the note and shoves it into her apron pocket. "Yes, that is good letter."

"Don't stop now, Mama," Mitzy urges. "What did she hear talk about?"

"It is nothing." Her mother picks up a knife and starts paring a potato. "Just mothers' talk. Asher, you read paper now."

"All right, let's see." I open the paper, dated October 1, 1888. "Measles reported in Staffordshire. Inventor behind aquarium craze passes on. Oh look, the Royal Court Theatre opens. Shall I read that one then?"

I spend the rest of the morning and half the afternoon at the table with them, which is fine and everything, but I can't get two seconds alone with Mitzy, and her mother won't let her out for a walk in the wake of the murders, so we don't get to strategize. Then Mrs. Kraskov pulls me aside. She tells me how Duvid sometimes comes home for a late lunch. How he doesn't want any boys near his "invalid" niece. How it would be best if I disappeared myself for the rest of day. How she's sorry to cut my visit short. Then she sends me off with a pocket full of walnuts and permission to come again.

So when are Mitzy and I supposed to talk, really talk? If she could see, then at least I could sneak notes to her sometimes. But this. This is hopeless.

Too frustrated to sit around in my own empty flat, I head over to the Cable Street vestry again. They still aren't letting anyone in, so I join the men outside the window. An old guy in a bowler hat tells me they're dealing with the second murder now. I listen in.

> Coroner: "Inspector McWilliam, based on your examination of the second victim, do you have any conclusions as to the instrument that was used?"
>
> McWilliam: "It had to be a sharp-pointed knife, at least six inches long, I should say. The kind of knife a butcher would use, perhaps."
>
> Coroner: "Now tell us about the apron."
>
> McWilliam: "Yes, we discovered a bloody scrap of apron farther down Goulston Street. The fabric matches that of the apron worn by the victim."
>
> Coroner: "Indeed. Now, tell us what you know about

the graffiti found near this bloody apron."

McWilliam: "On Sunday morning, your honor, I saw some fresh chalk-writing on the wall at Goulston Street. It said: 'The Juwes are not the men who will be blamed for nothing.' I penned a copy of it and gave instructions to have the graffiti photographed. But instead, the city police rubbed out the graffiti, saying it might cause a riot against the Jews."

So the graffiti was put there to blame the Ripper on the Jews. And someone else was casting suspicion on a butcher. It wouldn't be hard to connect the dots—to blame a Jewish butcher. I wonder if that's what's going to happen, or if that's what actually *did* happen, since this is the past. I don't know. We got all of about one sentence on the Ripper case in Western history class, and that was about how he might have moved to the U.S. after London. So yeah, I have no idea. All I know is I can't listen to another minute of this. I think I'll go walk Mum home from work.

7

I wait outside the matchstick factory, watching the workers spill out from their shift. Two girls in headscarves and short coats stop near me while one of them kneels to tie her boots.

"Hate the thought of that fiend using one of our matches to light his thieving candle," says the one who's kneeling over her bootlaces.

Her friend pulls a slice of bread from her coat pocket and takes a bite. "What you talking about, Mabel?"

"Weren't you listening to what Hettie was saying?" Mabel stands up and starts adjusting her scarf. "Them foreign criminals, they make special candles that put folks to sleep. So they can rob 'em easier, see."

"No!" The friend shoves the half-eaten bread back into her pocket. "That is terrible news." She slips her arm through Mabel's, and they start strolling. "Wouldn't mind using one of them candles on my poppa, though, when my Thomas comes to call."

Now I spot Mum. I give her an exaggerated smile to let her know everything is fine. But of course, everything isn't fine. Nothing is fine.

"Why aren't you at work?" she asks. "What's wrong?"

"Nothing's wrong. Mr. Diemschutz had to be at the inquest."

We head in the direction of home, not saying much, not saying anything at all really. It's dark now, and we both just want to get away from the horse smells, the damp air, the pedestrians shoving past.

"Brown bread and cheese for supper, I'm afraid," she says when we reach Berner Street. "I don't even have a vegetable."

"That's all right," I tell her. "Anyway, I have a few walnuts for you."

"Don't tell me you've gone spending your hard-earned pennies on treats for me."

"Think of it as a gift from Duvid Kraskov."

"A gift from…?" In the moonlight, I can see her raise an eyebrow. "You must have had one interesting day."

❧

I've barely taken my first bite of brown bread and cheese when someone is rapping at the door. Hard.

"Now who could that be?" Mum pushes back her chair, but I'm already up. I wonder if Duvid Kraskov somehow found out I was with Mitzy today. Maybe I left a footprint or a fingerprint or disturbed his newspaper.

I open the door, bracing for the ogre. But it's not Mr. Kraskov. It's two cops, their brass buttons gleaming on their navy tunics, their helmets strapped below their chins, their billy clubs at their sides.

"Good evening," announces the older one, a paunch-bellied man with red stubble on his face. "Is your father home, lad?"

Mum is at my side now. "I am a widow. What is this about, officer?"

"We're here to take a look at your rooms."

"Our rooms?" Her voice is stone.

"It's in connection with the murders, ma'am. We're doing house visits amongst certain East End dwellings, is all."

"Certain dwellings?" I ask. As if I don't know what he means. "Why is that, sir?"

"Asher!" Mum whispers sharply.

"It's all right, ma'am. The lad asked, and he deserves an answer. We have witness reports, son. People who say they saw the victims on the night of their murder, with a man who looked…foreign."

"Foreign?" I challenge.

"Yes." The officer clears his throat, averts his eyes. "Jewish."

His sidekick, a lanky, clean-shaven man, coughs.

"I see," Mum says, not sounding the least bit surprised. She steps aside to let them enter.

"But, Mum—"

She shoots me a warning look. "It's just this room and the one in the back."

The younger officer goes straight to the back bedroom. He's going to get on his hands and knees and look under my mother's bed for the murderer. Then he's going to rummage through her closet, handle her nightgown and her stockings, push aside her shawl and her one good blouse. I hate him almost as much as I hate the Ripper. Maybe more.

The older officer canvasses the main room, first squatting down to check under my bed, then opening the kitchen cupboard, as if the Ripper might be hiding where a few dishes barely fit. The cop's shoes clomp against the floor as he upends everything in the place. Just doing his job, just putting in another shift, then going home to—what?—a proper house with flowers in the box and meat on the table probably. I despise him too.

"Would you show me your knives?" the older one asks, still scanning the room. I go to the table and pick up the knife sitting next to the half-loaf of brown bread. "Is that all?" he asks.

"That is all."

The younger one emerges from the bedroom and gives his superior a quick shake of the head. The boss nods and turns to Mum. "Do you have any other lodgers, ma'am?"

"No."

"Have you had any lodgers in the past month?"

"No, it's only the two of us."

"Then we'll see ourselves out." He smiles stiffly. "Good evening to you."

The door rattles behind them. Mum stands there, glassy-eyed and pale, but I don't want to stand around for another instant.

"I'm going upstairs," I say.

"Upstairs, why?"

"To check on Maya and her mother."

"Who?"

"Maya Kraskov and her mother." I start buttoning my vest. "They moved in with Mr. Kraskov last week. They're up there alone now, and they might get worried when those policemen knock on their door."

I don't know how I know Mr. Kraskov works this late. Two days ago, I didn't even know who he was. But the longer I'm here, the more I become the person whose life I fell into. The more I become Asher. The less I remain Abe.

"Ash, no." She stands in front of the door.

"But—"

She folds her arms. "If the cops find you up there five minutes after they saw you down here, well, they're already suspicious. It won't take much to make them more so."

I have to admit it, Mum has a point. I can't help Mitzy tonight. Maybe I won't ever be able to help her. But I won't give up trying. I won't.

❧

"Abe?" The voice glides through my open window a few hours later, right after I get into bed.

"Mitzy, hi."

"Did you have visitors?"

"Yeah." I'm on my back, looking out the window, at the clotheslines and the fog. "Is it all right to be talking?"

"Uncle Duvid is snoring to raise the dead." Her window squeals as she opens it wider. "Mama's in the whatchama-callit—the water closet down the hall."

Which means we have to talk fast. "What was it like?" I ask. "With the cops."

"They just looked around. Under the bed and inside the closets."

I roll onto my side. "Same here. They made us show them our knives. Knife, to be precise."

She laughs a little, the first time I've heard her laugh since we've been here. Scratch that. It's the first time I've heard her laugh ever.

"Anyway," she says, "it's a good thing we never got hold of Papa's butchering knives after he passed, or they might think we're the culprit ourselves...oh, crap!"

"You okay?" I prop myself up on my elbow.

"Did you hear that, Abe? I just told you my father was a butcher. I know what he did for work, even though no one told me so. I just know."

"Yeah, me too." I sit up. "I mean, not about your father, but things. Things about me. About this me. Like I'm turning into Asher."

It's silent for a minute. When she finally speaks, her voice has climbed an octave. "Abe, we've got to escape before we forget ourselves."

"I know. Hey, do you remember our fifth-grade teacher's name?"

"What?"

"I'm just trying to make sure I have it right."

"Mrs. LeFay."

I sit up. "LeFay. So not DuBray?"

"Oh crap, you're right, Mrs. DuBray. How could I for-get—I loved her. I...school mascot. Tell me it's the silver fox."

"Yes. At least, I think so. Wait...maybe it's—"

"Hold on," she says, then adds in a hurried whisper, "Mama coming. Change the subject."

"Okay, all right." I drop onto my back. I might as well talk about the here and now, since I seem to know it better than Fort Pippin these days. "So, your father was a butcher."

"Yup, same place Uncle Duvid works—Greenblatt's. Papa was the one who talked Mr. Greenblatt into hiring him, back when Duvid first came to London the year before last." She stops short when she hears her own words, hears herself saying stuff she didn't know she knew.

"I know, weird," I say.

"Weird doesn't begin to cover it." Her voice sounds closer now, like maybe she's resting her chin on the window sill. "What was your father like?"

"My father." I rub my shoulder. "I'm pretty sure I idolized him when I was little. I thought he knew everything, could do anything. Then just when I was starting to work out that he might be a mere mortal, he came home from his job at the railway one night and never got out of bed again. Scarlet fever." Mitzy's right, I think, this is light-years beyond weird.

"That's..." She sucks in a breath. "Awful."

"Yeah." I move closer to the window. "What happened to your father?"

"An accident at work. He was helping carve up a side of beef, and his knife slipped, and he got cut."

"He stabbed himself?"

"No, not like that. Just a cut to his arm, nothing big or deep. He bandaged it up, switched out his knife, kept right on working." She makes a deep sigh, as if she's really remembering this stuff, as if she really feels the loss. "It must've gotten infected or something. The next day his arm swelled up, painful, and he ran a fever. He died that same week."

"I'm sorry, Mitzy."

"Yeah, me too. Abe?"

"Mm hmm?"

"Will you come up tomorrow?" she asks.

"If I don't have to work. Mitzy?"

"Mm hmm?"

"Next time your uncle is snoring, will you keep your window open?"

8

I push open the door to the Workman's Club this morning just as Mr. Diemschutz is emptying his tea cup. "Asher, you're here, good." He picks up one of the crates of jewelry sitting on a bench and motions for me to grab the other one. "Let's see how they took care of Polly in our absence."

We don't talk much as we walk down Berner Street. Mr. Diemschutz doesn't offer anything about the inquest, and though I'm dying to know what I missed, I don't know if it's okay to ask. The only boss I've had in my real life is my lawn-mowing gig with old Mrs. Gupta, and she is definitely not the type you'd ask a sensitive question. I decide to keep my mouth shut.

After a couple of blocks, we turn into a place called George Yard, where the ramshackle wooden horse stables come into view. I guess this is where Asher—the real Asher—likes to hang out on Sundays. Not me. At least, not yet.

"What day is it today, Asher?" Mr. Diemschutz asks.

"Wednesday, sir."

"Right, Mitre Square then. Let's hope the bad news hasn't dampened business there."

Mr. Diemschutz didn't need to worry. The square is thrumming with shoppers and hawkers, a congested, noisy horde of people and wares. Women carrying wicker baskets edge between carts and wheelbarrows that brim with vegetables, cloths, trinkets, and, in our case, cheap jewelry. Gaggles of kiddies dart in and out of the fray. A constable strolls by every so often, and so does an orange alley cat. The air smells like roasting nuts and fried fish and something else, something I eventually learn is a dish called pickled whelks, whatever that is.

"All right then." Mr. Diemschutz parks Polly and the cart in between a rag seller and a fruit cart. "Let's see if we can make up for lost time."

"Looks busy as ever," I say, even though I shouldn't know how busy it usually is here. I jump down and retrieve the jewelry crates.

Over the next few hours, we manage to sell several pieces, and my boss seems pleased. As for me, I'm mostly bored, but I remind myself it could be worse—I could be apprenticing for a leech collector or a sewer cleaner, after all.

When the bells toll one, Mr. Diemschutz tucks into the knish he brought along, and I pull out the crust of bread and chunk of cheese I packed. I spend the lull trying to spot the wall across the street where the chalk graffiti used to be, but I can't get a clear view.

After lunch, Mr. Diemschutz dusts off his hands and announces, "Look here, Asher, I have to see a few suppliers on Commercial Street. I think you're ready to run the show for a bit. What do you say?"

"Me? I, um…" Shoot, I should've paid more attention to how Mr. Diemschutz handled the cash.

"You'll be fine." He puts on his top hat and straightens his necktie. "You know just about everything there is to know by now."

"If you think so, sir."

"I'll be back by five."

And I actually am fine doing this alone. There's not much to it, as far as I can see. Just waiting around for someone to like one of the trinkets badly enough to part with her pennies. Watching out for sticky fingers. Making sure no one bothers Polly.

In the late afternoon, something starts to change, though. I can't put my finger on it exactly, but the mood in the square shifts somehow, and I start to feel uneasy. Maybe it's because more people are showing up, which is strange because this is the time of day when things should be winding down.

"How much is this?" a tired-looking woman asks, holding up an enamel brooch.

"Sixpence," I tell her.

"Don't suppose you'd let it go for three or four."

"I would if I could, ma'am."

She studies the pin, sighs, puts it down. "I'll ponder it while I shop then." She moves on, and I know she won't be back. But I'm not thinking about a lost sale. I'm thinking, Does this woman sense what I sense, that something is wrong around here? Could it just be me?

No, it couldn't.

Suddenly a voice rises up from the other side of the square. More voices join in. They're shouting something in unison, but I can't make it out. Polly starts to fidget, so I step over to her while I strain to hear. "Shhh now," I whisper to the pony. "I got you, girl."

Now the jumble of voices resolves into words. Angry words. Hateful words. I won't let myself believe it at first. I tell myself they're saying something about booze. But no, that's not it. The word is *Jews*. They're bellowing, "Down with the Jews!"

The rest of the square goes mute. A bunch of men—maybe a dozen of them—march around the square bellowing their insults. Then the onlookers join in—boys, women, children too young to know what they're saying. I close up the jewelry cart, but the crowd is too thick for escape.

Suddenly someone is talking at me directly. "Whatsa matter?" a husky voice spits from a few feet away. "Afraid to face your judgment?"

It's a kid about my age, but taller and broader, arms crossed. Two of his friends emerge from the crowd and plant themselves at his side. One of them has the sooty face of a chimney sweep. The other one, younger and barefoot, has a cigarette hanging off his lip. I move around from behind the cart and stand in front of the jewelry crates in some stupid protective stance.

Across the square, the mob chants, "It was a Jew! No Englishman did it!"

Closer by, the ringleader kid takes a step toward me. "Yellow belly, ain'tcha?"

"I'm not scared," I answer. "I'm just thinking."

The leader smirks. His sidekicks stare me down. "Go on, Lipski," the chimney sweep dares me. "Tell us what you're thinking."

"I was thinking how it's kind of funny." I take in a breath. "I don't know what this slum has more of, people or rats. But I do know which group you belong to."

As soon as I get the words out, I know what an idiot move it was. Verbal sparring with a bunch of roughs? Not my finest moment. And I'm about to pay for it. Maybe *I'm* the person who's going to die if I don't prevent it.

The chimney sweep starts forward, fists clenched. The smoker digs his bare toes into the ground and lets the cigarette fall out of his mouth, grunting some threat I can't make out. The ringleader tells them, "Stand back, mates. He's mine."

I couldn't run even if I wanted to, which I do want to. But I have Mr. Diemschutz's wares to protect. I have my job to protect. And, yeah, I guess I have my pride to protect too. So I ball up my hands and raise them in a pointless effort to shield my face. The leader is coming my way.

"Hoy, Ralph!" a man's voice shouts from behind me. The ringleader looks over my shoulder. "Come on," the man hollers, "we need you for the big show."

The ringleader—Ralph—bursts into a crooked grin. "Guess this is your lucky day, Lipski," he tells me. "Come on, mates!"

With that, he and his two accomplices dart past me to join the man. I finally lower my hands and pivot to see where they're going. But Ralph is wrong—this is not my lucky day. Just as I turn around, a hawker is shoving his cart along in an escape attempt. I take the corner of the cart on the side of my face, hard.

Fuzzy stars burst across the afternoon sky, and the coppery taste of blood dribbles into my mouth. Now there's a strange sound in my ear, but I don't think it's from this collision. No, it's coming from the mob.

The daytime stars follow my gaze across the square, making it hard to see. Finally, I zero in on a clump of men and boys carrying something over their heads. No, not something—someone. No, that's not right either. I blink and try again.

There, now I see. It's a mannequin dressed up to look like one of the Ripper's victims. She's wearing a dress stained with bright red splotches. Something like cherry jelly trickles from her lips. Her neck is bent at an odd angle. The mob shouts, "It was a Jew! It was a Jew! It was a Jew!"

"Yes, I'm sure I'm all right," I tell Mum as she holds a damp rag to my jaw. We're sitting at our table—well, I'm sitting, and she's constantly jumping up to see if the swelling is going down.

"When did Mr. Diemschutz finally show up?" She wrings out a fresh rag in the wash basin.

"Five o'clock, just when he said he would."

She shakes her head.

"It's not his fault, Mum. He didn't know this was going to happen."

"No, but I should have."

I take the rag from her. "How do you figure that?"

"I know more of the world, of people, than you and him put together."

I guess she's right—about me, anyway. I never knew the Jew-haters used the Ripper spree as an excuse. Most of what I know is from that one *Unsolved Mysteries* episode, which isn't much, just that the murders happened, that the Ripper got away, and that no one ever even figured out who he was.

"I cannot believe I let you go to Mitre Square so soon after." Mum rubs her forehead, then checks mine for fever. "I should have seen this coming. I should have."

"The police were the ones who should've seen it coming." I feel the anger rise inside me like fireworks. "They should've had more cops on the beat."

"Maybe." She shrugs. "Honestly, I don't know whose side the police are on these days. I guess I should just be glad you kept all your teeth."

I run my tongue over the inside of my bruised cheek and listen for sounds upstairs, for signs of Mitzy. Lowering the rag, I tear the crust off the slice of buttered bread in front of me. It hurts to chew, so I pop a small piece of the soft part into my mouth and wait for it to dissolve. What I really want is something cold, something like ice chips, but I'll have to settle for a cool cloth and a room-temperature lump of bread.

Now someone is knocking at the door. Great, what now? More cops? I start to get up, but Mum is already on her way. "Mr. Diemschutz, good evening," she greets him.

Somehow I know Mr. Diemschutz has never dropped in on us before. This can't be good. He was so quiet on the way home from Mitre Square, too. Maybe he didn't like the way I handled—or failed to handle—things today. Maybe he's here to fire me. Or maybe he's going to give up the jewelry business, now that it's dangerous. Crap. I'm sure he doesn't pay me much, but whatever the wage is, I know Mum counts on it.

"Good evening," he says.

She steps aside from the door. "Come in, please."

Mr. Diemschutz walks into the room, carrying something wrapped in newspaper. His eyes go straight to me, but he doesn't say hello. He doesn't say anything, just takes off his hat.

"Can I help you with something?" Mum asks.

"Hmm? Oh yes, yes. My Shaina, she made this for you. She hopes it will make Asher feel a little better. So do I." He hands Mum the package.

She tears off the paper, and the room fills with the scents of lemon and vanilla. "A sponge cake, how very kind. Please give her our thanks."

"I should not have left your boy alone at the square." He runs his hand over his black hair. "Asher, if you aren't well enough to work tomorrow…"

Wait, he's not firing me. He's apologizing.

"I'll be fine. I *am* fine." I walk over and extend my hand.

Mr. Diemschutz's hand meets my hand, but his eyes won't meet my eyes. "We stick together now. You, me, and Polly."

"See you in the morning, sir."

"I must be getting back to the club now." He puts his hat back on. "Good night to you both."

Good night? Ha. Not only can't I escape this place—I can barely survive it.

9

M r. Diemschutz takes one glimpse at my face the next morning and blanches. "Go home, Asher. Your face looks like chopped liver."

"I feel fine," I protest.

"That may be, but not a shopper in London will come near us with you looking like that."

That's what Mum said, but I don't want to lose another day's wage, seeing how I'm pretty sure I'm stuck here for a while, if not forever. "Isn't there something I can do?"

"I could use a set of hands right here," Shaina Diemschutz announces from the other end of the meeting room. "The charwoman went home yesterday with hives, and I've got to get this place ready for tonight."

So it's settled. Once Mr. Diemschutz leaves for the market at Bromley, Mrs. Diemschutz brings me a mop and bucket and the promise of potato knishes when they're ready. She shows me how to swab the floor and wring the mop, and then she heads to the kitchen to cook.

I settle into the dunk-swash-wring rhythm of my chore, pushing the mop under and around benches, watching the wood floor darken under the sudsy arcs. It's easy work, but by the time I finish, my jaw, my whole face, is throbbing, probably from having my head bent down for so long. When Mrs. Diemschutz catches a glimpse of me, she goes straight back to the kitchen and returns with a slice of hardboiled egg.

"Lucky for you I was in the middle of making egg salad," she says. "Here, use this on your eye right away. It will take the black and blue out. Go, sit."

"Yes, ma'am." I don't know how an egg is going to help,

but it does feel nice and cool against my swollen eye. I wonder how bad I actually look. Well, at least Mitzy doesn't have to see me like this.

"Ten minutes at least," she adds. "In fact, I have to run out. Why don't you go home and lie down for an hour?"

❧

Mrs. Kraskov cringes when she opens the door for me. "Oy-yoy-yoy, what happened to you, boychik?"

"What's wrong?" Mitzy asks from her perch at the table.

"I got caught in some trouble at Mitre Square."

Mrs. Krasnik's eyes balloon. "We heard about riot—you were there? *Oy vey iz mir.*"

"Asher?" Mitzy says, and she sounds, I don't know, concerned, I guess. Which, I confess, is kind of musical to hear.

"I'm fine," I tell her.

"Let me see for myself." She holds up her hands and wiggles her fingers.

I glance at Mrs. Kraskov and go to the table. Mitzy scoots closer and finds my neck. Slowly, she moves her hands up to my jaw, my chin, my lips. "Does this hurt?" She runs one finger over my nose.

"Not at all."

She touches my cheekbones, my temples, my eyes. Her hand stops when it reaches my left eye, still swollen almost shut. "I think Mama is the only one here with two working eyes."

Mrs. Kraskov pushes aside the walnuts on the table and produces a raw potato and a paring knife from her apron. "I make, how you call, remedy." She cuts off a slice of potato and hands it to me. "Here. Hold to eye. Will make better."

Mitzy sniffs the air. "It smells like potatoes."

"To make the *shvarts*—the black—go away," her mother explains.

"Um, thank you." I put the potato slice over my injured

eye, although I'm pretty sure it won't work any better than Mrs. Diemschutz's egg. "How long do I keep it here?"

"One quarter hour," Mrs. Kraskov instructs. "And again little later."

Mitzy picks up her nutcracker and a walnut. "Mama, isn't Mrs. Graham expecting you?"

Mrs. Kraskov nods. "Family down hall has baby," she tells me. "I hold him, help out when I can."

"Happy to keep Mitz—Maya company," I say. "I have an hour."

"You are good boy, Asher." She sets the paring knife down and pushes her chair back. "Maya, you be careful, yes?"

"Yes, Mama."

As soon as Mrs. Kraskov is out the door, I shove the potato slice into my vest pocket and pick up the spare nutcracker.

"Abe, what happened to you?"

"The riot." I crack a nut and toss the meat into the bucket on Mitzy's lap. "I was there selling jewelry, and I ran into a cart someone was trying to push out."

"Great." She props her chin on her hands. "I'm blind, and now you have a job that gets you knocked around. How're we ever supposed to get out of here?"

"Let me ask you something, Mitz." I take a breath. "Have you, has this ever happened to you before?"

"Has what ever happened to me before?"

"This. Time travel. Space travel."

She lets out a little snort. "Are you implying that I'd fall for this scam twice?"

"No…"

"Why, has it happened to you?"

"No, but I was thinking." Through the wall, two high-pitched voices tell us someone is having a spat in the flat next door. "Last year, you were out of school for a while. A long while."

"What about it?"

"Well, no one ever said where you were." One of the intruding voices gets louder, then a door slams, and it goes silent. "I was wondering if maybe you were somewhere else then, somewhere like this."

She shakes her head and smiles a little, but it's not a happy smile. "No, Abe. I wasn't out combing the space-time continuum. I was out having thyroid cancer."

My nutcracker hits the table with a thud. "I...Mitz, I'm sorry. I didn't...didn't know."

"Nobody did. I wanted it that way." She plays with the collar of her blouse. "I wanted to slip out, get treated, slip back."

I can tell she doesn't really want to talk about it, but I can't drop it like it's nothing, I can't. It's a huge thing. Life altering. "So did you, like, have an operation? Chemo?"

"Yup, and my hair came back blue."

She says it so deadpan, I don't know how to react, so I sit there like an idiot.

"Relax, Abe. I didn't lose my hair. I just decided to wear it blue after that. Like, in your face, cancer. Like, this is my body, and I'm the only one who gets to mess with it."

"I like it," I say.

"Which—the color or the attitude?"

"Both."

She slides her hands over the walnuts on the table, pushing them this way and that. "Well, if we ever get out of here, maybe I'll switch it up. Purple or fuchsia or something."

I have no idea what fuchsia is, but I'm sure she'd kill it. "You know what else I was thinking about?"

"What?"

"Remember when you got that red letter *T* for our presentation about Saturn?" *Please let me be remembering this right. I need that memory to be real.*

"Yup."

"You stole that, didn't you?"

"I like to think of it as borrowing," she says.

I wince. "Tell me you didn't get caught, didn't get in trouble for it."

She presses her temples, like she's trying hard to summon the memory. Then she sits up taller and says, "Didn't get caught. I only had it for a couple of days anyway. I bet no one even noticed."

"I noticed it."

"You did?" She sounds surprised.

"Yeah, I was out on my bike the very next day. I passed the TOUCHLESS CAR WASH, except it was the OUCHLESS CAR WASH."

"But…" She looks confused. "I don't think that's right. Wait. Yeah, I took the T from that old boarded-up ice cream shack in Hadley——Pete's."

"So you made it Pee's?"

"Yeah…I think. The more I focus on it, the blurrier it gets."

"Well, it sounds like you. You're bad." I say it jokingly, trying to cheer her up a little. But she doesn't smile back. She's not anything close to smiling.

"Well, maybe this is my delayed punishment." She picks up a nut. "Or maybe this is one giant punishment for all the bad things I've ever done."

"I don't think that's how the world works, Mitz."

She turns to me, her brown eyes flashing. "Then how does the world work, Abe? Take a look at where we are, you and me, right this very minute, and explain to me how the world works."

When I don't answer—how could I possibly have an answer?—she fills in the blank. "Never mind. Besides, if I really thought this was a punishment, then I'd have to believe it's a punishment for you too. I'd have to believe that Abe Pearlman colored outside the lines somewhere along the way. Which is impossible."

This is not a compliment. This is not even a simple observation. It's a judgment, a label.

"What do you mean?" I ask. A stupid question because I know exactly what she means. She means I'm a geek, a bit of a loner, and athletics are not my strong suit. That much I remember loud and clear. I don't need to make her say it out loud.

"Come on, Abe. Did you ever, I don't know, bring home a bad report card?"

Sigh. "No."

"Miss curfew?"

"Nope."

"Keep a library book out past its due date?"

"Nada."

"Yeah," she murmurs. "Me either."

She says it like it's a confession, like it's a secret. Which is amazing because it means she's letting me in. She's telling me she's not the bad girl everyone assumes she is. Mitzy Singer is letting me in, even if it's just a little. She's not looking through me or ignoring me. She's telling me her truth, and that makes it perfect.

"I, um, thanks," I fumble.

She shoves her hair behind her ears. "For what?"

"For, y'know, sharing."

"Oh." She shakes her hair back out, freeform. "Well, don't get used to it."

Too late, I want to tell her. *I'll never get un-used to it, to knowing you.* But I don't say it. Instead, I push back my chair. "I have to get back to work."

A corner of her mouth lifts in a smile. "Who's going to buy jewelry from a face like that?"

"No one. I'm working for the boss's wife at the clubhouse today."

"When do you get off?" she asks.

"Don't know. I—I can call out my window when I get home. Leave your window open if it's safe?"

" 'kay."

I set down my nutcracker and stand up. "See ya," I say, which might just be the stupidest exit line on the face of the planet.

10

After I wipe down the insides of the meeting-room windows, Mrs. Diemschutz has me slicing onions in the kitchen while she kneads a ball of dough. Tonight there's going to be music and a lecture about fair wages. They're expecting a crowd, and the crowd will be expecting refreshments.

"Is this enough?" I ask.

"Do a couple more. This will be supper for half of them." She starts mashing a pot of boiled potatoes, adding salt and heaping spoonfuls of schmaltz—chicken fat. After a while, she dips a fork into the pot and takes a taste. "You can add the onions now."

I dump the bowl of onions into the pot, and she stirs them in, along with more schmaltz, some spices, and two eggs.

"Good. Now to roll out the dough." She sprinkles flour on the table, then she takes out her rolling pin and molds the dough into a long sheet. "All right, now spoon the potato filling on top."

"Do you always make this much food?" I ask as I work.

"Yes and no." She folds the dough over the filling, then crimps the seams shut. "We always offer refreshments, but the truth is, I'm worried folks might be afraid to come here after that terrible business in the yard, so I'm sweetening the pot a bit."

"Well, they say the Ripper never strikes the same place twice, so that makes the club about the safest spot in town."

"I suppose. I'm just not sure people look at it that way." She steps back to take in her work. "I'd say this is ready for the oven."

I nod. "What's next?"

"The cakes." She tightens her apron strings. "But that's a snap. Why don't you call it a day. Carry these glasses into the meeting room on your way out, would you?"

"Yes, ma'am." I pick up the tray of glasses and head into the main room, my mind far away. Well, not so very far away—just a couple of blocks away, to Mitzy. Still, far enough that I don't notice the other person at first.

Duvid Kraskov. He's sitting alone on the last bench, his chin down as if he's sleeping or praying, I can't tell which. But why? It's the middle of the day. He should be at work. Besides, there's nothing going on at the club until later tonight.

"Mr. Kraskov?" I venture.

He glances up, clearly surprised to see me. "What happened to you?" he grunts in Yiddish.

"I, uh, got caught at Mitre Square." I run one finger along the tray. "Is everything all right?"

"Am I not allowed to sit here?" he accuses.

"No, no. I mean, yes. But usually you're at work, aren't you?"

"Work is *fercockt*—screwy—today. So I'm taking it off."

Mrs. Diemschutz walks in carrying a tray of spoons and forks. She stops short when she sees the newcomer. "Oh, good afternoon," she says in English. "Are you here for the lecture? It's not until seven o'clock, I'm afraid."

"I think he just wants to see the place," I offer. "He's starting English lessons here next week."

"I see." She switches to Yiddish now. "Well, welcome. Stay for as long as you like."

Something is wrong. Duvid wouldn't skip work on a whim. He wouldn't show up at a social club on a lark either. He's the kind of man who works all day and goes straight home for the night. I somehow know that about him. So what's up? Did he lose his job? Is he ill? Is he hiding? I better find out.

⁊

I run straight from the clubhouse to Mitzy's flat, where Mrs. Kraskov is standing over a boiling pot and Mitzy is stirring a bowl of beet salad at the table. They're in business-as-usual form, like nothing out of the ordinary is going on. Which means they're clueless about Duvid.

Maybe I should tell them where he is, but I don't. Something tells me not to. Besides, maybe there's a simple reason he skipped out on work. Maybe he needed a mental health day. Maybe he'll come home at his regular time, and everything will be fine. I can always hope, can't I?

No, as it turns out, I can't. I'm not there for five minutes before there's a knock at the door. Mrs. Kraskov answers it. Two police officers and a man in a business suit—a detective?—stand there, grim as the Reaper.

"Wh-what is it?" she stumbles.

"Is this the residence of Duvid Kraskov?" asks the man in the suit. He's got sandy hair parted in the middle and an upturned mustache.

"Something has happened?" Mrs. Kraskov frets. "He is hurt? He is…?"

"Not at all, ma'am," answers the poker-faced suit. "We would just like to talk to him. Is he in?"

"He is at work. What is the matter? Please, I worry."

"May we come in for a moment?"

"Yes, yes." She holds the door open, and they file in.

"Ma'am," the suit says, "we are inspecting the knives of slaughtermen in the area. In connection with the murders."

"What is this—slaughtermen?"

"*Shochets*, Mama." Mitzy rises from her chair, but I take her elbow and coax her back into her seat.

Mrs. Kraskov's mouth falls open. "Duvid? No, not Duvid. He is, how you call, homebody. He never. He would never."

"Just the same," insists the suit. "Are any of his knives about?"

"We just told you, he's at work," Mitzy snaps. "With his knives." She gets up and finds her way to her mother. I join her.

The suit tilts his head and makes a small cough. "It would seem that he is not at work, miss. It would seem he fled the slaughterhouse as soon as I showed up to perform the inspection."

Oh, crap. This is not good. This is bad, really bad.

"Fled," repeats Mrs. Kraskov. "You mean, run? No, no. He has nothing to hide. He, he get scared, that is all. He has not the English. He not know what you say."

"Even so," says the suit, "I'd like my men to have a look around. Do you mind?"

"I..."

"Thank you, ma'am." He nods to the uniforms, who set off checking under beds and inside cabinets. Again.

"Your men already did this," Mitzy flares.

"Yes, doubling back is an inevitable part of a thorough investigation." The suit scans the dingy room. "Now, you wouldn't happen to know where Mr. Kraskov might have gone today, do you?"

"No," Mrs. Kraskov answers. "He free to go where he wants."

"And you, young lady? Any ideas?"

Mitzy shakes her head.

"What about the lad?" he asks.

"He's just our neighbor," says Mitzy. "He only got here five minutes ago."

I don't know whether to tell them what I know, but I don't trust these men, so I keep my mouth shut. We stand there until the two uniforms finish their search, empty-handed.

The suit motions his men toward the door. "When you do see Mr. Kraskov, would you please let me know? Detective Stuart Barker. You can leave a message for me at the Cummins Road station."

Neither Mrs. Kraskov nor Mitzy responds.

"Right then, we'll see ourselves out." The detective and his men file back out, and it feels like they take all the air with them.

It's horrible holding on to a secret this big, a secret that feels more like a ticking bomb. I loosen my top shirt button and wipe the sweat off my neck. Fort Pippin never felt as far away as it does right this minute.

Mrs. Kraskov starts pacing and wringing her apron. "If Duvid leave work, why he not come home? Why he run in first place? What he is hiding?"

Mitzy laughs out loud. "Mama, you don't actually think he's the Ripper, do you?"

"Of course not. But he is hiding *something*." She stops pacing. "I will go looking for him."

"No, don't," I say, more sharply than I intend. "I mean, you don't have to. I know where he is."

"What?" they both demand.

My hands are clammy. So are my armpits. "He's at the Workman's Club. At least, he was there half an hour ago."

Mrs. Kraskov's mouth drops open, her eyes burning. She's mad at me, or at Duvid, or maybe she's just confused, or maybe she's scared. Then she shakes it off, the confusion, the fear, the whatever it is she's feeling. "I must go there." She reaches for her coat on the door hook.

But there's another knock at the door.

It's one of the uniforms who were just here, a skinny guy with a sunburned face and a ginger beard. "Ma'am, I'm here to inform you that we've just intercepted Duvid Kraskov."

"What means intercepted?" She glances at me and then back to the uniform.

"He was walking in as we were walking out," explains the cop. "We're taking him to the station for some questions."

"I do not understand." Her voice cracks a little. "What questions? Why him? Why Duvid?"

Mitzy takes her mother's hand. "Do you think my uncle is the fiend, sir?" She says it calmly, matter of factly.

"No one thinks anything at the moment, miss." He scratches his beard. "We're simply looking for some facts."

"He will not understand your questions," Mrs. Kraskov insists. "He does not have the English. I told you that."

The cop nods. "Worry not. We have officers who know French, Spanish—"

"Yiddish?" she barks. "Your officers, they know Yiddish? No, I must go. I speak for him."

"I'll do it, Mama." Mitzy holds her mother's hand a little tighter. "It will be easier. I have more English than you."

"No, Maya. I mean…" She lets out a loud sigh. "*Oy vey iz mir*, I do not know. Okay, all right. We both go. Where? Where we go?"

"I will escort you," the cop offers. "It's not a long walk, just over to Cummins Road."

"My daughter, she is—"

"Yes, I know, ma'am. We'll take it nice and slow."

"I'll come along too," I finally speak.

The cop looks over at me, as if he hadn't realized I was in the room. "How's that, lad?"

"It is all right, Asher," Mrs. Kraskov says. "Duvid would not want anyone else there."

Mitzy nods in agreement, but we all know the truth of it: Duvid would not want *me* there. Still, what if he's the guy I'm supposed to save—save from false accusations, from jail, from hanging? What if he's the person in the prophecy?

11

It was awful," Mitzy tells me afterward. It's just the two of us in her kitchen. Her mother has gone for a lie-down. Her uncle is behind bars. I want to take her hand, but I don't because, well, because I'm the loser who doesn't have the guts, even after all we've been through together.

She props her elbows on the table, sending a few walnuts skittering. "They brought us into a room at the back of the police station. It was small, I could feel it. Cold, too, and it stank of tobacco. We sat at a table with that detective guy—Barker, whatever his name is."

"A nice cozy chat?" I scoff.

She rolls her unseeing eyes. "He said something like, get Duvid to talk or else. Then they brought him in. In shackles. I could hear the clinking. They think they've got their man."

But have they got *my* man? Is Duvid the person I'm supposed to rescue?

"Tell me what happened." I drum my fingers on the table. "Tell me everything."

She scratches her forehead. "Well, Mama lit into him before he even sat down. In Yiddish, obviously. Duvid, tell me what's going on, she says. Duvid, they think you're the Ripper."

"And?"

"And he doesn't say a word." I slump back in my chair. "Then I gave it a whirl. Just tell us where your knives are, I tell him. They only want to look at them, not take them away from you. I begged him to spill. Not a peep."

It's funny, in a way. I think of myself as pretty creative, pretty good at coming up with stories, putting characters in strange situations and figuring out how they get from point A to point B. But for the life of me, I can't come up with a single reason Duvid would do this to himself. I can't deduce, induce, reduce, introduce, or produce one reasonable explanation. Maybe I'm trying to apply logic where it doesn't belong. Maybe this is beyond reason, beyond sanity even.

"Then Mama got a little hysterical," Mitzy goes on. "Shouting. Jumping out of her seat. Slapping the table. You're just making yourself look guilty, she hollers. I know you aren't a killer, Duvid. We all know it. You just need to prove it."

"Let me guess," I say. "More silent treatment."

"No, he finally decided to speak." She rubs her eyebrows, exhausted. "He said, it must be getting late, Bina. You should take Maya home."

"Fool."

"And then something really weird happened." Mitzy lowers her voice. "Uncle Duvid started to cry."

Wow, I didn't think the guy had it in him. Emotion, I mean. Other than anger, that is.

"And, Abe." She touches my arm. "Don't ask me how, but I knew he'd never cried in front of anyone before. Not even when Papa died. I knew it to the bone. And now there he was, weeping."

I decide here and now that Duvid Kraskov really is my man, that he's the one I need to rescue. I only wish I had the slightest idea how to do it.

Mitzy takes her hand off my arm. "Listen, whatever he's hiding, it's important. To us, I mean. I can feel it. We have to find out what he's covering up."

"Okay, all right." My fists are on the table. "Let's take it on then. Let's look for his knives. Or go at Duvid from a different angle. Hit him where he lives."

She nods and tucks one leg under her. "Barker said maybe

Duvid will think better of it after a night in the pokey. That's what he called it—the pokey."

"Maybe he's right."

"Or maybe Uncle Duvid will rot in jail."

"No. No way," I say. "Not going to happen."

"You don't know that."

She's right. I don't know anything. I don't know if we'll get out of the slum, or if Mitzy will get back her eyesight, or if we'll ever eat crappy school cafeteria food again. All I know is that I can't sit here and do nothing.

"Look, I have an idea." I finger-comb my hair. "I'm going to try talking to Duvid myself."

"Abe, he wouldn't even talk to his own family. Why would he talk to you? You're a stranger."

"Maybe that's the point. Maybe his relatives are the last people he'll tell his secret to." I hadn't thought of this before, but now it kind of makes sense. "Maybe a stranger is exactly what he needs."

"But—"

"What've we got to lose?" I say.

"He could get upset with you for butting in, that's what."

"He's already upset with me, Mitz. Just for, y'know, existing." She makes a little snort through her nose. "Am I right?" I ask.

"I guess, yeah." She untucks her leg. "Listen, Abe?"

"Uh-huh?"

"I just, I…this is off topic, but…" She pulls at a loose sleeve thread. "What do you think about when you walk the track before school every morning?"

Wait, she's seen me? I didn't think anyone, least of all Mitzy Singer, had noticed me. Not ever, and especially not at seven in the morning. "I, uh, it's not very interesting."

"That's what people say when they're hiding something interesting."

I look around for an escape hatch. Surprise, there isn't one.

"And you promised, no secrets."

"You really want to know?" I cringe. "Okay, all right. It's how I get ideas for my stories. I, yeah, I write short stories." There, I said it.

She tilts her head at me. "And you get new ideas by walking the same quarter-mile loop every day? Looking at the same old soccer field and bleachers?"

"It's not that. It's not the scenery exactly. It's the walking, I guess, the moving, the quiet. It just works for me."

"Hmm." She moves to the edge of her chair. "So, ideas just pop into your head when you're out there?"

"Sort of."

"Tell me one. Tell me an idea you got on the track." Now she's putting me on the spot. She's asking me to set one of my creative seedlings on the table. No one has ever asked me to do that before. "Unless it's too personal," she adds.

"No, it's okay." Nerve-racking but okay. "Right now, I'm working on a story about...about..." It's on the tip of my tongue. I can almost taste it, it's so close. *Think, think.*

"Gone?" she asks softly.

"Ye—no, I have it. It's about a town where the flu is going around. Except that instead of making you sick, this flu makes you smarter."

"Uh-huh." She's really listening, I think. Like she's, I don't know, interested in what I'm saying. Like she cares about what goes on inside my head. Which is weird—mind-blowing, actually.

"So everyone's trying to catch this flu," I say. "Only, no one knows how long the smarts last. Or what happens to you down the road. Or...well, that's as far as I've gotten."

"Cool." She's drawing little figure eights on the table with her finger. "The writing, the walking, the ideas. I like it."

"Thanks," I mumble, still feeling blown away. "So. So anyway, what do you think about when you sit on the memorial bench after school every day?"

"Absolutely nothing—that's the whole idea." She closes her eyes and touches her hands together namaste-style. "Clearing my mind. Keeping the world out of my head for a few minutes, you know?"

"Yeah, I do." I smile a little bit. "That's what the track is for me. No people, no house noises, no traffic lights. Empty space, free for ideas to drop into."

She opens her eyes. "I wish an idea would drop into our heads right now."

"Me too."

She doesn't say anything after that, and I can't think of anything to say, and the silence is starting to feel a little awkward, or a lot awkward. I mean, where do you go with a conversation after you've shared all this private, serious stuff? You don't start talking about the weather or tomorrow's lunch menu, you just don't.

"Anyway, it's time for me to get going." I push my chair back a couple of inches. "Tomorrow I'll—"

"Abe." She grips my arm. "Abe, listen."

"Okay." I move my chair back in.

"The reason I never say anything when you walk past me on the bench every day." She clenches me a little tighter. "The reason I don't say hi back."

"But I don't say hi."

Her forehead wrinkles. "What?"

"There's nothing for you to say hi back to. I don't say hi in the first place."

"You don't?"

I shake my head. "I can only get up the nerve to nod." Another crystal-clear memory.

"But...oh." She sounds baffled, like she can't understand why someone like me would be nervous about talking to someone like her. "Okay, fine. The reason I don't nod back. It's because I'm afraid."

This makes me laugh. "You, afraid of me?" There's no

universe where a Mitzy Singer should be afraid of an Abe Pearlman. Not this Abe Pearlman, and not the billions of Abe Pearlmans in all the parallel universes that might be out there. It's ridiculous.

She loosens her hold on me. "Not afraid *of* you. Not you as a person. I'm afraid—ugh, how do I say this?"

"Just say it."

"Okay, all right." She fidgets in her seat, like she can't find a comfortable position. "I'm afraid if I do something nice for myself—make a friend, have some fun—if I tempt fate, then my cancer will come back. Just to show me who's boss." Her hand slides away as she droops back into her seat.

So Mitzy is afraid she's going to die. And she's afraid to live. What a terrible place to be. I clear my throat. "Another case of 'I don't think that's how the world works.'"

"I know, I'm stupid."

"No, you're brilliant." And then I do something bold before I have the chance to change my mind. I put my hand on top of hers. Which may not be much in the big picture of bold romantic gestures, but it's freaking audacious for the likes of me.

She doesn't take her hand back. Maybe she's too sad to pull away—sad about the cancer, about being afraid, about being blind. But maybe, just maybe, she kind of likes the way my fingers feel on hers.

That's all that happens tonight. It feels like a lot. I've shared some stuff with Mitzy. I've sort of held her hand. Yeah, that's plenty for one night. Besides, I need to save what's left of my chutzpah if I'm going to confront Duvid tomorrow.

12

You'll be glad to know my charwoman is back today," Mrs. Diemschutz tells me the next morning. We're in the clubhouse kitchen, and she's standing over a basin heaped with dirty plates and glasses from the night before. "No washing or scrubbing for you today."

She's going to set me loose early—perfect. I can go straight to the police station, to Duvid.

"They could use a hand in the back room, though, I bet," Mrs. Diemschutz adds.

"The back room?"

"It's the print shop for our newsletter."

"But I don't know the first thing about running a printing press," I say.

"Don't worry, the fellows will show you what to do." She pulls a dish towel off its rack. "Go on now. It's right behind the stage."

Okay, all right, maybe this won't take all morning. How long could it take to run off a few pages? "Yes, ma'am."

Now someone is calling from the front room. "Hello? Anyone here?"

Mrs. Diemschutz frowns. "That must be the coal man. He's early today." She heads out to the front room with me at her heels.

It's not the coal man. It's a repairman who's come to fix a leak in the roof. He rubs his Mr. Clean-style bare scalp with one hand and his roly-poly belly with the other. He is in the middle of introducing himself when the clubhouse door flies open.

"Missus D, Missus D!" the charwoman pants, an empty laundry basket on her hip. I recognize her from the day she ran into me with her pipe. "There's a bald-head tub o'lard walking around like he's casing the joint and—oh, hello, mister." She smiles sweetly at the repairman. "Top of the morning to you."

"Thank you, Christina," Mrs. Diemschutz says through gritted teeth.

Then another man comes out from behind the stage to say the printer is on the blink, so they can't run the pages. Suddenly everyone is talking at once. In the hurly-burly, I duck out. *Hurly-burly*, sheesh.

Mitzy did a good job the night before describing the police station interview room. It's cramped, stuffy, smelly. The chairs are crooked. The table has a big crack down the center. And I don't even want to guess what those dark splotches are on the floor. Luckily, I don't have to wait long. I barely park myself when Detective Barker walks in. I stand up.

Barker leans against the wall, stroking his waxed mustache. "Good morning to you, lad."

"Good morning."

He checks the slip of paper in his hand. "I understand your name is Mendel, Asher Mendel. What brings you here today?"

Desperation, I want to say, but I don't. "I told the man out front, sir. I'd like to see Duvid Kraskov. I think I can get him to talk."

"I appreciate the gesture, young man." Barker gives me a forced smile. "But we've been trying to get him to talk since yesterday afternoon. His family tried too, till they were blue in the face. His boss was here earlier. What makes you think you can do any better?"

"Because," I say, "whatever it is he's hiding, he's hiding it from *those* people. He's worried what they'll think about him. Me? He doesn't care one crumb what I think."

"Huh." Barker crosses his arms and gives me the once over, like he's trying to decide whether I'm a complete idiot or possibly kind of clever. He brushes his chin with his thumb and shifts his weight.

"Ten minutes, sir. Give me ten minutes with him, and if I can't make any headway, I'll leave." Barker has a *no* poised on his lips. "Five minutes," I try again. "A one-off. I won't come back again, I swear."

Barker looks at the floor and shakes his head. "You're wasting your time, lad."

"Maybe, but—"

"You're wasting my time too." Then he shrugs and looks up, a little brighter. "But since we're both here, I suppose we can throw another few minutes at it." He goes to the door. "Stay right here."

A quarter hour later, Barker returns. He doesn't say a word to me, just stands there holding up the wall like before. Soon a cop walks in, escorting a shackled Duvid Kraskov.

The hair on my nape stands up. I've never sat down with Duvid before. I've never talked with him for more than a moment. And I've never had the feeling that my entire future—and possibly Mitzy's—rests on one conversation. I swallow hard.

"*G-gut-morgn*," I stumble.

Duvid sits across from me at the table. His black and silver stubble somehow emphasizes the dark circles under his eyes. He's got bread crumbs on his rumpled shirt, and his fingernails are cracked and broken. The two of us have a stare-down for about six seconds, then I have to look away. When I look back, he's still staring, unblinking, and this time I force myself to hold his gaze.

"Mr. Kraskov, please, tell me," I say in Yiddish. "Tell me what happened, so I can tell the cops. It's your only way out of here. I won't breathe a word to Maya or her mother, I promise you."

He's listening. He's thinking, too—I can almost see the cogs spinning in his head. But I have no idea *what* he's thinking. Let's face it, I've never been the most intuitive duck in the pond, and this guy is a whole different species of bird. All I can do is sit and wait, so I do. Time stretches out like an endless sky.

Finally, he leans forward, dropping his elbows onto the table. "You? I'm supposed to trust *you*?"

"Yes. Yes, you are."

"Ha!" He shoves his chair back with a squeal.

"Who else are you going to trust?"

"No one," he spits. "And especially not you."

"Why do you think that?" I hear my voice rise. "Why especially not me?"

He points to his head. "Because I know what goes on up here with you. You only want my niece. You hoodlum you, trying to act like the hero."

Great. I guess the long night in the pokey didn't do squat.

"Besides," he mumbles.

"Hmm?"

"If I tell you, then you'll tell the cop." He moves his chair back toward the table. "And how do I know this *fercockt* cop won't turn around and tell my family?"

"I—I can ask him about it," I offer.

Duvid rolls his eyes.

"Mr. Kraskov?"

"Go on then," he says. "Ask."

"Yes, okay." This feels like progress, I think. Maybe Duvid really will talk to me if he just gets some reassurance. I turn to Barker. "Sir, Mr. Kraskov will tell me his story if you promise the information won't leave the station. Can you swear to that?"

"Certainly," says Barker.

"Good, thanks."

"As long as his testimony doesn't lead to criminal charges,"

Barker adds. "If formal charges are made, then it becomes a matter of public record."

"Well?" Mr. Kraskov asks me.

I turn to face him, take a breath, nod. "The detective promises." It's not that I'm lying. It's that I can't believe it will go any other way. Duvid Kraskov, the Ripper? No way.

Duvid bears down on me again with those unswerving eyes. "And you, you must swear on something. Swear on something when you tell me you will not tell a soul." His voice is a hard rock of misery. "Especially not my family."

"On...something?" I look around the table, the room.

"On your father's grave," he presses. "Swear to me on your father's grave."

I wonder how he knows about my father. Not that it matters, but still. Maybe Mum told him. Yes, that must be it. Before I blew into this world, she must have said so. "I swear. I swear on my father's grave."

Duvid makes a grumbling sound that I take for approval.

I cough dryly. "On one condition."

If he looked angry before, he's raging now. I can see a vein throbbing in his neck. His pale face has turned brick-red. He's at his wit's end. I actually feel bad for the grouch, but that won't stop me from making my demand.

"My condition." I clear my throat. "My condition is that you let me see Maya freely. I can visit at your place. Take her out. See her freely."

He lowers his head like a bull about to charge. Raises his shackled hands to his face. Lowers them. Takes in a breath. I've got him in a corner, and he knows it. I just don't know whether he's going to save himself.

"So...?" I urge.

"So, you take my Maya out, and then what—you tell her everything as soon as you're out of my earshot?"

"No!" I lie.

"How do I know you won't?" he growls.

"Because I swore on my father's grave. Because I wouldn't do that. That's not who I am."

"Don't piss on my back and tell me it's rain, boy." His words are gruff, but his voice is tired, papery.

"Is that a promise then?" I ask. "A promise that I can see Maya freely?" I don't know what I'll do if he says no, so he'd better say yes.

"Fine already. A promise."

"Good. Then I also promise. I promise I won't tell anyone. But there's one more thing I want."

His eyes constrict into snake-like slits. "Now you know how much trouble I'm in, you are suddenly the hard bargainer. What do you want now—my job, my right arm?"

"I want you to learn English."

"Learn English?" He sounds almost amused. "Now you care about my education?"

"No, I care about your ability to understand what people are saying behind your back. Our backs."

"I tried learning. The clubhouse was closed down."

I lean forward. "Well, it has opened back up." I make myself hold his stare. "I want you to learn English."

He looks over at Barker, then down to his shackled wrists, and lets out a long sigh. "Is that everything, this time?"

"That's everything."

"All right then, agreed."

"Good. I'm ready to listen now."

He sits up a little straighter, trying to rub the back of his neck, which isn't easy with the chains. "Did you know I used to have a brother?" he asks, and so his story begins.

My brother, Yosef. Maya's father. Bina's husband. A good man, smart too. Smart with his hands and his head both. He was younger than me by two years, but he always did things better. We both trained to be *shochets* at the same butcher in Russia. I was all right at it, but Yosef was born for it. Every slaughter quick and painless. I have two left hands by comparison, if you want to know the truth.

Yosef and Bina were matched when he was twenty. They married, had a baby, the way it's supposed to be. We all lived together in the same house, my mother too. I watched Maya lose her eyesight, a little bit each day. It was a terrible thing. By the time they left for England, she was completely blind. They asked Mama and me to go with them, but Mama wouldn't leave the place where our papa was buried, so I stayed too.

Five years later, I buried Mama. Measles. Suddenly I had no reason to stay in Russia, and plenty of reasons not to. I came to London to be with my only remaining family. Yosef helped me get the job at Greenblatt's. Helped me get the room on Berner Street. He even tried to help me learn this crazy tongue you use here. I was content.

I was content for many months, a year maybe. Then one day at Greenblatt's, Yosef and I were out back with an animal. Yosef did the killing, a beautiful job, the beast didn't feel a thing. Now it was time to open it up, take out the *treif*—unkosher—parts and examine the organs. We were working together on it, and somehow—I don't know how, I wish I could remember—my blade nicked Yosef's arm.

We keep our blades so sharp, it barely takes a tap to make a cut. This is not to make excuses, but to tell you it didn't take much to split his skin. It wasn't a deep wound, no heavy bleeding. He just washed it off. We thought that was the end of it.

My brother didn't let Bina or Maya know how he got the cut. He let them think he did it himself with his own knife. Why let a little spilled blood turn into bad blood, he said. The cut would be healed in a few days' time anyway, he said. But the cut didn't heal. It festered.

Turned bright red. Oozed. Then the fever. The sweat. The shaking. Then he died.

I did not, could not, would not, let Bina or Maya know how Yosef got that cut. I still cannot. I will not.

Now you're thinking I am a selfish fool. It's true, and there's more yet. Listen. When we were sitting shiva, I heard Mr. Greenblatt talking to Bina. He said Yosef left his knives at the slaughterhouse his last day of work, the day he went home early with fever. Mr. Greenblatt promised to get the blades to her for a remembrance. That's when I butted in to say I'd deliver the blades to Bina as soon as I returned to work.

But I didn't return those knives. I kept them for myself. I kept my brother's blades for my own remembrance. They were all I had left of him. Two knives with the initials YK carved into the handles. I needed them like my lungs need air. Understand me—I would do anything for Bina and Maya, but I could not hand over my brother's blades. Besides, how could I ever use my own knives again, the knives that cut Yosef, that killed him?

Bina—I made excuses. I told her the blades got misplaced, that I'd look for them at the slaughterhouse every day, that as soon as they showed up, I'd bring them. She said it was all right. She didn't really want a reminder of the thing that killed her husband. Mr. Greenblatt—he was easy. He never had to know what happened to the knives once he handed them over. He just assumed I gave them to Bina. Why wouldn't he? So I got what I wanted without very much trouble.

I used Yosef's blades every day, doing the work he could no longer do. When Bina and Maya moved in with me, I hid the knives under my bed at night. And so it went. I needed that part of my brother. I still do.

Then this detective here ruins it all. He decides the

Ripper is a Jew, a Jew with a sharp blade, so he turns up at Greenblatt's and wrecks everything. Because if I show him my blades, he'll see that the initials don't match my name. He'll ask me about it. Mr. Greenblatt will know I lied to him. He might fire me. Then Bina and Maya will find out—Mr. Greenblatt will tell them, or the detective will tell them, or someone else will tell them, and I'll lose them too.

For all I know, they'll pick up and move to America. They have cousins there, you know. They are my only family, but I am not theirs, you see. They have the luxury of options. I have only them, and only this job.

So I made a run for it. Stupid, I know. But once I started running, I couldn't turn back. I ran all the way to the Workman's Club. The place was already scoured inside and out after the courtyard murder. I figured the police wouldn't be searching there again anytime soon, so it was a safe place to hide the blades. I buried them under one of the shrubs in the back. Then I sat inside the clubhouse because I knew the cops would be waiting for me at the flat. I sat there for hours, until it dawned on me that I couldn't stay away forever.

Now here I am, confessing every detail of the story I wanted so badly to keep secret. What else can I do? So go ahead, tell this tale to that man in the corner. As long as Mr. Greenblatt doesn't find out. As long as Bina doesn't catch on. As long as Maya never knows.

"We'll have to keep him here until we retrieve his blades," Detective Barker explains as he walks me up front. "If the knives check out, he's a free man."

"Thank you, sir." I'm all formal and serious on the outside, but on the inside I'm whooping for joy.

After we shake hands, I step out onto Cummins Street and fly back to Berner Street. I have so much to tell Mitzy.

13

As soon as Mrs. Kraskov opens the door for me, I know I've walked in on something. She's got her coat on, misbuttoned, and Mitzy is standing behind her in warrior pose. They aren't yelling or even talking, but the tense-o-meter is through the roof.

"Um, hello?" I step inside.

"Asher, Asher," Mrs. Kraskov gushes. "You just in time."

I look from her to Mitzy. "For…?"

"For to keep Maya company," she says. "I am going back to station. Talk some sense into Duvid. He acting like crazy man."

"I still think I should go with you," Mitzy argues. "I have more English. For translating to the detective."

Mrs. Kraskov shakes her head strenuously. "I tell you before. I think Duvid is, how you say, embarrassed—embarrassed for to explain in front of you."

I could settle this tiff right now if I tell them what I know, but a promise is a promise. I'll tell Mitzy later, of course—I have to believe she'll be leaving this place before long, after all. But Mrs. Kraskov will still be here with Duvid, and I need to keep my secret. I almost give Mitzy a quick thumbs-up before realizing what a stupid mistake that would be.

"Mama—" Mitzy tries again.

But her mother is already in the doorway. "I come home soon as I can. With your uncle, God willing." And she is gone.

Mitzy paces the apartment while I explain everything to her. By the time I finish, she's red-faced and starting to breathe hard. "They'll let him out as soon as his knives check out?" she asked.

"That's what they said."

She stops burning a path in the floor. "Then you've saved his life, just like Zinnia ordered. You can go home now, Abe. Back to the twenty-first century. That's..." and here her voice cracks. "That's fantastic."

"Don't worry, Mitz, I won't go without you. You'll get your boat ride—Zinnia said so. And I'll wait here till you do."

"I doubt you can decide when to leave." She rubs at her knuckles. "I mean, we didn't get to pick what time we came here, did we? Zinnia didn't ask us whether it was convenient to get ripped away that very minute, did she?"

Mitzy's right, as usual. We turned up in London immediately after Zinnia read our cards. No running home to pack a bag, no jotting off to 7-Eleven to get snacks for the road. And definitely no putting it off for a couple of weeks, or even a couple of days. So maybe I'll blow back to Fort Pippin as soon as Duvid walks out of that jail cell. Maybe Mitzy *is* going to be here alone. My belly swarms with hornets.

"Hey, let's go somewhere," Mitzy says. "For when it happens, for when you leave. Let's go up on the roof."

"The roof?"

"We can be alone up there." She finds my arm. "That way, no one will see you if you vanish into thin air."

The hornets jostle and bump in my stomach. "But how would you get back downstairs?"

"It's just one flight. I'm getting used to feeling my way around. Besides, I need air." She pulls me in the direction of the door. "Come on."

"But..." I start, then lose my train of thought. "All right."

We climb the fire escape up to the roof, which overlooks laundry lines and the street below. It's chilly up here, and the roof is covered in soot and bird droppings, but it smells better than on ground level, plus it's nice and quiet.

We walk laps around the roof for a while, talking about everything and nothing really. Mitzy wonders if Asher has discovered computer games and Netflix yet. I ask what Maya could be making of all those holes in her ears. We laugh a little. A nervous laugh. I can't even say what games I own anymore, and she can't tell me how many ear piercings she has. Or used to have.

Then we sit down with our backs against the chimney and don't say much. We've been up here more than an hour now, according to the church bells. I wonder if there's a problem at the police station. Maybe the cops couldn't find the buried knives. Maybe Duvid is making more trouble.

"The moon is out," I tell Mitzy.

"Mmm."

"Some stars too."

"How many?"

"Oh," I sigh, "somewhere between two dozen and a hundred million, I'd say."

She lifts her head as if she's looking up at the night sky, as if she can see the stars and the moon. Then she closes her eyes and murmurs, "I shall be laughing in one of those stars."

"What?" I ask.

"It's from *The Little Prince*. Have you read it?"

"Uh-uh."

She smooths her skirt and resettles herself. "Well, in the story, the little prince—he's from outer space—he's saying goodbye to the pilot he met in the Sahara. And that's what he says—'I live in one of those stars, and I'll be laughing down at you.' Something like that."

I look up at the Milky Way.

"Then the little prince adds, 'So whenever you look up at the night sky, it'll seem like all the stars are laughing.'"

"A sky full of laughing stars," I muse. "Nice parting gift."

"Yeah."

This talk about parting makes me think of Mum, of wanting to say goodbye to her, of wishing I could leave her a note. But what would I say? What could I possibly say to her that would make a shred of sense? Besides, once I'm gone, the real Asher will probably be back, so it won't be a goodbye for her at all.

"Want to hear something eerie?" Mitzy asks.

"I'd love to."

"This morning when I woke up." She scoots away from the rough bricks of the chimney. "For the first time ever, I knew right where I was, no surprise. I didn't think I was in Fort Pippin. I didn't have to adjust. For the first time, it was almost like..."

"It's going to be okay, Mitz. You're going to get home."

"Do you really think so—or do you just hope so?"

I don't answer her. Because that's when I see them, Duvid and Mrs. Kraskov, walking slowly down Berner Street, their faces unmistakable in the moonlight. Duvid is free. He's almost home. And I'm still here. I feel all my muscles constrict. "Mitz-Mitzy..."

"Uh-huh?"

"Your mother and uncle. They're home." Funny, as I say it, my muscles relax. Because I don't want to leave Mitzy alone up here on the roof. I don't want to leave her at all.

We get to Mitzy's flat a few minutes before her family walks in. Duvid looks spent. He doesn't say a word, just drops onto his bed in the main room and turns toward the wall. Mrs. Kraskov looks bewildered, like she can't understand why the cops suddenly changed their minds and let him go. She probably doesn't know whether to feel glad for him or furious with him. Probably both. Plus, she's worried about my being in the same room as the overly protective uncle.

"Asher," she whispers, nodding toward Duvid. "Maybe not good time now. Maybe not best mood."

Then Duvid calls out in Yiddish, "Asher, help Maya and her mother shell those walnuts, will you? They're piling up."

Mrs. Kraskov stands there open-mouthed. Now she's really baffled. Duvid was actually inviting the no-goodnik to spend time here. "Perhaps tomorrow," she says. "It is late now."

"Fine," he grunts.

Emboldened, she adds, "I like give some to Mrs. Graham tomorrow. Her children maybe like."

"We'll do it right now," Mitzy says. "Ash, grab the bucket and a nutcracker."

As soon as we get out into the hallway, Mitzy bends over, fists on her knees, gulping for air. "I can't, I can't do this anymore, Abe." She puts her hand to her belly and squeezes her eyes shut. "I can't be here. I can't be blind. I can't!"

I set the pail down and put my hand on her shoulder. "You won't have to, Mitz. You're going to get out. As soon as you take that boat ride."

She straightens up and faces me, her cheeks burning. "You mean, the same way that saving Uncle Duvid from hanging got you out?"

"I...look, maybe Duvid never would've hanged anyway. Maybe he's not my man, and that's why I'm still here. I really think—"

"Never mind." She fans her flushed face with her hands and takes a deep breath. "Let's unload these nuts. Where's number forty?"

"Mitzy—"

"I'm tired, Abe. Let's just do this."

I tap at number 40. We hear voices, but no one answers our knock. I'm just about to rap again when the door opens, and a plump woman in a headscarf appears, a baby on her hip. Behind her, the room bustles with kids, and they're not using their indoor voices.

The woman breaks into a toothy smile when she sees Mitzy. "Hallo, sweets. I've been hoping to catch ye. Tell me…" She glances at the noisy crowd in her flat and decides to step out into the hall with us. "Good evening to you too, lad."

"Hello."

She lowers her voice. "Tell me, dove, is it true?"

"Is what true?" Mitzy asks.

The baby starts tugging on Mrs. Graham's headscarf, and she bats his hand away. "About your old man getting nibbed, o'course."

"Nibbed?"

"Arrested, love. Say now, do they really think he's the Ripper?"

Mitzy clutches. "How do you know my uncle got arrested?"

"Why, everyone knows." Mrs. Graham shifts the baby to her other hip. "Everyone in the building, anyway. He got picked up right here, now didn't he?" She turns to me and offers a conspiratorial wink. "I'm Ida Graham, by the way. Mrs. Ida Graham."

The baby starts to fuss and kick, his bare feet thrusting into Mrs. Graham's apron. His face turns red, like he's getting ready to belt something out at the top of his lungs.

"Alma," Mrs. Graham calls over her shoulder. "Alma Mae! Come get Archie. For heaven's sake, he's hungry."

A girl comes forward and relieves Mrs. Graham of the unhappy baby. A toddler is holding the girl's skirt in one hand, a beat-up rag doll in the other.

"Go on now, Alma Mae," Mrs. Graham scolds. "Shoo."

The girl throws us a weary glance and retreats.

"Now don't you worry, poppet," Mrs. Graham tells Mitzy. "No one's going to hold any of this against you and your mum, no matter how it turns out. There's only so much us ladies can do to keep our men on the straight and narrow, after all." She makes a clucking sound with her tongue. "Ain't I right, honeycomb?"

Mitzy's mouth drops open.

"We brought you some walnuts," I say, because this conversation really needs to end. I hand her the pail.

"For me? Why, isn't that kind of you, lad."

"It's from Maya and her mother. Oh, and here." I pull the nutcracker out of my vest pocket. "You'll need this."

"That Missus K is so kind to us," Mrs. Graham says. "So very kind, even in her time of sorrow."

A racket bursts out from inside the flat, the high-pitched voices of squabbling brothers and sisters. Mrs. Graham cranes her neck around and shouts, "You fopdoodles best pipe down unless you want to see the backside of me hand!" When she turns to us, she's smiling sweetly again. "Perhaps I should be going, lamb. Give my best to your mum, won't you?" The door snaps shut behind her, and the yelling starts back up.

"This is our life now," Mitzy informs the door. "Our existence."

"She's just an old gossip, Mitz."

"Yup, just like everyone else. Like every other person in this miserable city." She turns her back to the door. "In this whole lousy world."

Think, think, think. Think of something to make her feel better. But there's nothing, because what she's saying is true. Unless we can break out, this is our life.

"Walk me back, Abe." Mitzy's voice is scratchy, like sandpaper against wood, like she's too tired to talk.

I take her hand. Maybe things will look different tomorrow. Maybe some sleep will give us inspiration—if either of us can get any sleep, that is. I have a feeling it's going to be a whole lot of tossing and turning. That's what happens when you know the sun is going to rise in the wrong year, on the wrong city, over the wrong life. You spend all night thrashing around, not understanding, not wanting to be here, afraid you're slipping away from the real you, worried that if enough time passes you won't even remember where you were born, where you belong. You agonize that you'll wake up one day thinking this is where you're from, where you fit, where you need to stay.

It's enough to make your head blow up. *Tick, tick, tick, ka-boom.*

14

Duvid has been out of jail for a week now, a bleak, endless week. Mitzy and I trudge through the days pretending they're normal ones, but nothing is even close to normal, and we don't know if it ever will be. All I can think about is how we may never get home.

At least I had a shorter work day today. Mr. Diemschutz and I went to Penwick Street market, which closes at noon, so now I have the afternoon off. I go straight to Mitzy's, of course. When I get there her mother lets her take a short walk with me, as far as the nearest vegetable stand.

I've got Mrs. Kraskov's shopping basket on one arm and Mitzy on the other as we head down Berner Street. The afternoon is crisp and breezy, almost cold. It'll be chilly in the unheated flat tonight, but at least the streets stink a little less in this weather. That's something, anyway.

We pass a clot of kiddies trying to sell rags and whatnot out of wooden crates. Up ahead, one especially scrawny girl is using a stick to stir what looks like a bucket full of laundry. Next to her lies the crumpled coat rack I once saw hanging out of a window. Another rotten day in the slums.

"It happened again," Mitzy says.

"What did?"

"This morning in line for the loo." She clasps the collar of her coat when a gust of wind blows in. "I heard some girls talking about this year's Swan Upping, and I knew what it meant."

"What is it?"

"Every summer, they count the swans on the Thames River. Like a census." She shivers. "Freaked me out."

We skirt around a broken cart wheel. "Sort of like how I

know how to make change for a guinea. I actually know how many shillings are in a guinea. What if I forget how many cents are in a dollar?"

"Or what peanut butter tastes like," she adds.

"Or what I did for my birthday last year. Or my street address. Or who I am—I mean, who I was."

"I'll help you remember who you were."

"Thanks, Mitz." I look over at her, at her windblown hair, her nose gone pink in the autumn chill. "But you don't really know who I was before."

"Then tell me. Tell me who you were. Tell me what you did for your birthday last year."

"Um, okay." This is kind of embarrassing, because I didn't do anything for my birthday last year. I stayed home, like I always do.

"Abe?" she urges.

"I...uh."

"Did you already forget?"

"No, I remember." I readjust the shopping basket on my arm. "My mother made spaghetti and meatballs and cupcakes. Yellow cupcakes with chocolate frosting. We ate dinner, and then I did homework. Doesn't get much lamer than that," I admit.

"Oh yes, it does." She pulls a handkerchief from her coat pocket. "If it'll make you feel any better, I'll tell you what I did for mine. I told a fortune teller I wished I never had to lay eyes on another algebra problem again."

I stop in my tracks. "For real?"

"Happy birthday to me. Oh, are we here?" she asks.

We're just a couple of steps from the outdoor vegetable stall. "How'd you know?"

"I could smell it. Next thing you know, I'll be echolocating." Which sounds an awful lot like giving up hope. I guess I'll have to hold on to the hope for both of us, for now.

At the stall a man in an apron and derby hat is holding

court with a woman who wants to know why the green cabbages look purple. Her little boy is touching all the apples.

"What are we getting again?" I ask.

Mitzy loosens her hold on my arm. "Two onions, half a dozen potatoes, and a beet if they have it."

"Right." I put two large yellow onions into the basket. The woman with the cabbage problem points a finger at the vegetable man now, and her voice rises. I lean into Mitzy's ear. "Looks like this guy could use some rescuing. Think he's my man?"

"Not funny," she whispers.

"Sorry."

"No, you're not."

She's right, I'm not, because if I can't find something, anything to laugh at, I'm going to start crumbling. I move on to the potatoes. They all look like they've seen better days, or maybe they've never seen a good day, but slum dwellers can't be choosy, so I load six of them into the basket.

Suddenly Mitzy gasps and grabs onto me. I look down to discover a fat tomcat brushing against her skirt.

"It's just a cat, Mitz." I don't tell her the cat has a pigeon in its jaws.

"What color is it?" she asks. "Not black, right?"

"Don't tell me you're superstitious." She doesn't answer. "It's not black," I assure her. "It's gray, the kind of gray that would probably turn white after a couple of baths, so don't worry. I don't see any beets, though."

We have to wait awhile for the cabbage woman to finish her tantrum, then we pay. As we head back down the road, I ask myself the same question I've been asking since Duvid got released. Could I get used to this? If I had to, could I get used to living in this here and now, eating brown bread and cheese every day, eking out a living selling cheap costume jewelry, knowing I'll never see my parents or school or a hot shower again?

Of course I could. People have lived through a lot worse. I wouldn't like it, wouldn't choose it, but I could survive it. After all, my job isn't horrible. I like my mum. I'm even getting used to herring and black bread. What I couldn't stand is if Mitzy had to get used to it. If she had to get used to being blind for the rest of her life. Blind and miserable and caged in the room upstairs. As much as I like how we're friends here, I couldn't live with that.

"You're quiet all of a sudden," she says.

"Hmm? Oh, yeah. Just thinking."

"About?"

"I..." I rearrange the vegetables in the basket, stalling for time. "I was thinking about how the Ripper hasn't struck in a while. Wondering if he's done now. Wish we could Google it—the date of his last crime."

Her shoulders rise and fall. "Wish we could phone a librarian."

"Or watch a History Channel documentary about it."

"Or go to a museum with an exhibit on Victorian England," she says.

"Or walk into Mr. Wu's history class and ask him."

She tries to laugh, but it comes out like a groan. We don't talk much the rest of the way back. We don't talk much while we hang out at her flat, either. It's another endless afternoon.

And then there's the night to get through. The night of lying on that sagging bed, looking out at the fog pressed against my window, still thinking. Thinking of what Mitzy and I talked about today, what we didn't talk about. Of the way she smiles and the way she frowns. Of what it would be like to spend time with her in Fort Pippin. Would she still like me in the then and there?

Finally I roll over and go to sleep because I've got a long day of work ahead of me. Another endless day in the here and now.

15

Two days later it's Sunday, and it's just Mitzy and me, out walking, going nowhere in particular. We've made a pact that this afternoon we absolutely will not discuss our Situation. We're going to try to enjoy this day, this outing, this not having to sneak around behind Duvid's back anymore.

We wander from Berner Street onto crooked Stonecastle Road, zigzagging our way to Wimple Place and around to noisy Chiltern Street. We pass tenements and poorhouses, old ladies and street urchins, garbage and more garbage. The sky is thick with clouds, the wind is frosty, and the streets are jammed, but we're together, and who knows, maybe we're actually on a date. Whatever a date is.

Now we turn onto Dorset, a narrow street lined with rotting brick buildings and shadowy alleys. Most of the places here have been carved up into cheap shops or rooms for rent. It's ugly and run down, like all these streets. And everywhere you look, you see only one color, a color like a muddy raincloud, like grimy ash, like this corner of the world has given up on everything but gray.

Oh, but wait, what's this? Something different, something out of place. Something cheery. There, through the window of a grocery shop, a smiling woman is pulling toffee.

"Let's stop in here." I open the shop door, and we duck inside.

"Welcome to McCarthy's." The stout woman behind the counter doesn't look up from her candy-making. "I be Mrs. McCarthy."

Mitzy closes her eyes and inhales. "I smell butter. Mmm, and molasses."

"The lady is making toffee," I tell her.

"Toffee?" Mitzy lights up. "Tell me how she does it."

"Um, all right." We walk closer to the counter. "She has a big baking tray with a heap of toffee, and it's steaming hot."

Mitzy nods.

"She's rubbing butter all over her hands. All right, now she's digging into the toffee and picking it up."

Mrs. McCarthy looks to me and then to Mitzy. It takes her a minute, but she understands what's going on and holds her hands a little higher so I can get a better view.

"Now she's pulling, Mitz."

"What do you mean, pulling?"

"Here, I'll show you." I bring her hands together in front of her. "Imagine you're holding a big lump of toffee. You're gripping both ends tight, okay?" Then I pull her hands in opposite directions. "The toffee stretches out like a rope, like a long, sticky rope."

Mitzy laughs.

"Now she's folding the rope in half. And stretching it out again. And again."

"How many times?"

"Oh, I'd say ten or fifteen," Mrs. McCarthy pipes in. "Till it gets stringy and you can see it shine."

"It smells awesome," Mitzy raves.

"How's that, love?" Mrs. McCarthy asks.

"Wondrous," Mitzy corrects herself. "It smells wondrous."

Now another customer walks in, a woman with red hair long enough to sit on, and she's wearing black skirts under a white apron. "Afternoon, Mrs. M.," she chirps.

"Hello there, Mary Jane." Mrs. McCarthy keeps pulling the toffee. "What can I do for you?"

"It's me birthday today," Mary Jane tells her. "Twenty-six."

"Twenty-six already?" Mrs. McCarthy tosses the toffee onto the counter with a thump and picks up a knife. "You don't look a day past twenty-one."

Mary Jane produces a lopsided smile. "You are too kind, you is. Anyway, I decided to treat meself to a new candle."

"Help yourself." Mrs. McCarthy nods to the shelf behind her. "You can leave the half-penny in the till."

"Certainly." She heads behind the counter and pushes the candle into her skirt pocket. "I'm off to the Ten Bells for a celebratory pint," she tells Mrs. McCarthy. "Care to join?"

Mrs. McCarthy shakes her head and starts cutting the toffee into pieces. "You run along, Mary Jane. Have yourself a pleasant birthday."

"I plan to." She winks. "Ta-ta."

When the birthday girl is gone, Mrs. McCarthy leans over the counter at us. "Say, how would you young'uns like a little taste? A gift from your new friend." She cuts two bite-sized chunks and hands them to me.

"Thank you, ma'am." I give a piece to Mitzy and pop the other one into my mouth. Delicious.

"Nothing to it," Mrs. McCarthy says. "Just be sure to tell everyone where you got it. McCarthy's."

We're still chewing when we get outside. I put my sticky hand in Mitzy's, and we start to walk. It's snowing a little, and the wind nips our faces.

"That was fun," she says.

"Yes, it was." Who'd have guessed we'd ever actually have fun here. In the slums. In 1888. In Ripper country.

At the corner we turn off Dorset Street. It's starting to get dark out, and the gusts are more frigid by the minute. "Winter all of a sudden, huh?" I say.

"Are you cold?"

"No," I answer, which is an obvious lie, because my jacket is more holes than wool.

"I'll be the judge of that." She stops, lets go of my hand, finds my face. Her fingers touch my ears, my nose, my cheeks. Then she frowns. "You're freezing. Let's get you home."

Home. Mitzy called our tenement *home*. A hundred tiny

goblins jump up and down on my chest. Maybe she didn't really mean home—maybe she just meant the place we're staying right now, temporarily. Or maybe she did mean it. Maybe she's forgetting that we don't belong here, that we need to escape, that our real home is in another century on another continent.

"Come on." She gives my arm a little tug. "Mama will worry."

By the time we get to the tenement it's fully night, and the snow is beginning to collect in the doorways and alleys. The gaslight in the stairwell isn't working—again—so it's slow going up to the top floor. Finally, we make it to the third story.

"Well, hello there, ducks." Mrs. Graham, the next-door neighbor, is coming out of her flat as we hit the landing.

"Hello, Mrs. Graham," we say.

"Fancy running into you. I was just returning your bucket." She holds up the walnut pail.

Something smells strange, and I think it's coming from the bucket. I can't place it, but it reminds me of Mitre Square, the day of the riot. Something like vinegar and salt.

"I brought a little treat, as well." She steps forward. "Didn't want to return this empty."

I look into the pail and see a bunch of brown puckered lumps.

"It's wrinkles, them is." Mrs. Graham beams.

Mitzy sniffs. "Wrinkles?"

"Wrinkles, love. Pickled whelks."

Pickled whelks—that's it. Whatever whelks are. Mitzy doesn't know either, and she gives a little shrug.

"Sea snails," Mrs. Graham explains. "I thought your mum might like them for tea tonight. Try one now if you like."

Mitzy presses her lips together. "I'm sorry, Mrs. Graham, we can't eat those."

"The brine doesn't sit with you, eh?" She nods knowingly.

"No, that's not it," Mitzy says. "We're not allowed to eat them."

Mrs. Graham's forehead creases, then the lightbulb goes on. "Oh yes. You mean, on account of you being sheenies, is that it?"

For some reason, I want to laugh. Mrs. Graham has no idea she's insulting us. She thinks she's being understanding, maybe even respectful. Mrs. Graham is one of the nice ones, and even she calls us names. It's almost funny, in a pathetic way.

Mitzy doesn't think it's one bit funny. Her cheeks are bright red, and this time it's not because of the weather. It's because she's fuming. She opens her mouth, closes it, curls her lip.

"Am I right?" Mrs. Graham asks brightly. "It's one of them sheenies laws?"

"Something like that, Mrs. Graham," she manages through clenched teeth.

Now the door to Mrs. Graham's flat flies open, and a small boy appears. He's holding up his too-big short pants with his pudgy little fists. "Mummy! Alma Mae says she's going to toss me out the window if I snitch about—"

"Get inside, Simon," Mrs. Graham shushes.

Simon's face falls. "But she already got the window up, Mummy."

"I said, get inside," she scolds. When the boy finally retreats, she turns back to us with her most syrupy smile. "I guess I'll be popping back in then, doves. I'll fill 'er with something better next time."

She heads inside, calling over her shoulder to us, "Maybe a nice bit of blood sausage, how's that?" The door closes behind her.

Blood sausage.

Mrs. Graham says blood sausage, and just like that, instead

of almost laughing, I'm holding back a sob. Don't ask me why. I'm just tired, I guess, and confused.

"Abe," Mitzy says when she hears me snuffle, "what's wrong?"

"Nothing." I wipe my eyes.

She slips her hand into mine. "It's such a secret place, the land of tears."

"Hmm?"

"More *Little Prince*."

"Oh. Yeah, something like that."

My head swims with all the things I want to say to her. I want to tell her that I'm not keeping any secrets from her, not unless they're secrets I'm keeping from myself too. I want to tell her how courageous she is, how I hate this every bit as much as she does, how I've relished getting to know her these past weeks. But I don't say any of these things out loud. Instead, I hold her hand a little tighter and lead us down the hall to her apartment.

16

I sleepwalk through my day today. Dreamwalk, more like it. Envisioning pulled toffee, cheerful shopkeepers, snowflakes. From the barely dawn hour I wake up, to the long day at the Tilsbury market, through the rickety ride back to Whitechapel, I daydream about my day out with Mitzy. I don't really wake up until I get back to the tenement, to Mitzy's flat, and Mrs. Kraskov hands me the evening newspaper.

"'Fiend Strikes Again,'" I read the headline out loud while Mitzy, her mother, and her uncle crowd around me at the kitchen table. I pause for Mrs. Kraskov to translate for Duvid.

"Go on," Mitzy urges me.

"'The latest tragedy took place last night on Dorset Street.'" I glance at Mitzy.

Her eyes widen. Dorset Street. Toffee, Mrs. McCarthy's. And now the fiend.

I take a breath, then continue reading. "'This morning, the landlord came around to collect back rent for Miss Mary Jane Kelly.'"

Mary Jane Kelly. Could it be the same Mary Jane we saw yesterday—the birthday girl, the red hair, the half-penny candle? Did I miss another chance to save someone from dying? A scream forms in the back of my throat. I swallow it down and force myself to keep reading.

"'Failing to get any answer by knocking, the landlord went to the window, which had been broken and patched by rags for some time past.'" I read the words slowly to give Mrs. Kraskov time to keep up with the translating. "'On pushing the rags aside, it became evident to him that the police must be alerted.'"

Now Mrs. Kraskov starts tapping her wedding band against the table, first lightly, then harder, like a drumbeat. Mitzy takes hold of her mother's hand and whispers something soothing in Yiddish.

"'Scotland Yard's hopes of catching the fiend rose when one George Hutchinson, who had known the victim for some years, saw her walking home with someone last night,'" I go on. "'Hutchinson testified that he saw a man with a…'" My voice trails off. I cough, clear my throat.

"Man with a what?" Mrs. Kraskov asks. "You say man with a…"

I look to Duvid, who's studying the hair on the back of one hand. "'A man with a Jewish appearance,'" I said. "'The witness said he saw a man with a Jewish appearance enter her rooms.'"

Mitzy drops her chin. Her mother stares at her wedding band as she turns the terrible words into Yiddish. Duvid balls his hairy hand into a fist.

"Should I keep reading?" I ask.

"Go on, Asher," Mrs. Kraskov says.

So I do. "'The police place great reliance upon Hutchinson's description of the fiend, believing that it will enable them to run him down.'"

I drop the paper. No one speaks or budges for a long moment. Then Duvid pushes his chair back and reaches into his vest pocket. He pulls out a stone the size of a plum and turns it over in his hands.

"That explains this then," he mutters.

"*Vas?*" asks Mrs. Kraskov. "What is this?" He answers by rubbing the side of his leg. "Someone threw at you?" Mrs. Kraskov's voice shakes.

He stands up, walks to the door, and takes his jacket off the hook. "I'm going for a turn around the block."

"Duvid, no." Mrs. Kraskov jumps up and meets him at the door. "Don't go. It's not—" The door shudders behind him. Mrs. Kraskov comes back to the table and falls into her seat. "We must do something." Her voice is tight, her words clipped. "It is Russia all over again."

"Mama—"

"We cannot live this way, Maya. We must do something."

"Like what?" Mitzy cries. "What can we possibly do?"

Her mother reaches into her apron pocket, where something makes a crinkling sound. She withdraws a folded sheet of note paper—it's the letter from her cousin Annie, the one she read out loud to Mitzy and me. "We could go to New York."

What?

"America," Mrs. Kraskov says. "Live with Annie."

New York. Mrs. Kraskov wants to pick up and move to New York. She wants to separate Mitzy and me by the length of an ocean. I look at Mitzy. Her cheeks go white and then pink and then splotchy. I wait for her to fight this, to tell her mother no, she won't go, she can't go. But she doesn't say a word. She just sits there.

"But what about Duvid?" I blurt out. "What would he do without you?"

"Duvid come too," Mrs. Kraskov says. "That is whole point. He more safe in New York. He can find work there and be more safer."

Mrs. Kraskov leans back in her chair and looks off into nowhere. She touches her wedding ring, her hair, her collar. She's seriously considering taking Mitzy three thousand miles away from me, possibly forever.

"Mrs. Kraskov." I have no case to make, but still I try. "How could you afford passage?"

"I get something for ring." She twiddles her band. "And for my mother's."

"It won't be enough," I insist. Silently, I beg Mitzy to help me out here, to come up with a reason for staying, to convince her mother.

"No, not enough," Mrs. Kraskov relents. "But Duvid, he has topaz belonged to his mother."

"He does?" Mitzy finally speaks.

She nods. "It is what you call—oy, I have the word—keepsake. A keepsake."

I feel the color leave my face. I feel the air leave my lungs. Because I can feel Mitzy leaving me, slipping out of arm's reach, out of earshot, out of sight. "Do you think Duvid would ever agree to this?" I ask hoarsely, trying to keep the panic out of my voice.

Mrs. Kraskov opens her mouth to speak, but Mitzy beats her to it. "Why not?" she asks. "He left Russia to be with us. He can leave London too."

I wrack my brain for something to say, something to bring Mitzy back to her senses. Finally, I turn to her mother. "You probably don't want to rush into this," I tell her. It's all I can think of.

"I not rushing," Mrs. Kraskov says. "I am thinking about this since Maya lose father. And now the fiend, the Ripper. And there is something else besides—"

"Something else?" Mitzy asks.

Her mother unfolds the letter. "Something else Annie say."

All at once, I remember how Mrs. Kraskov stopped reading Annie's letter out loud that day. How she broke off in the middle of a sentence and put the note away. How I barely noticed it then. How it sickens me now.

Mrs. Kraskov turns to the bottom of the note. Softly, so softly I have to lean in to hear her, she reads,

> Before I close, I want to tell you something exciting I heard talk about. Something perhaps wonderful. There is talk about the American cure—the American cure for blindness. They say doctors have restored eyesight to the unseeing. They say only a few patients have been

treated so far, but it is happening. I think of your Maya, and my heart leaps.

"But…" I start. Could it be true? No, no way. If they'd found a cure for blindness back in the 1800s, I'd have learned about it in history class. Besides, the cure would still be around in the twenty-first century. No, Annie has heard false rumors, that's all. This is fake hope—and a terrible reason to take Mitzy away.

I clear my throat and try again. "How could that be so?" I ask. "The whole world would have heard about it by now. It's probably just—"

"Probably just a few patients treated so far, it is so new." Mrs. Kraskov stands up from the table. "I need think. I, yes, think. Excuse me." Before I can say another word, she hurries to her room and closes the door behind her.

The second I'm alone with Mitzy, all the words burst out. "Mitzy, you know that cure doesn't exist. Why are you agreeing to this—why do you want to move to the other side of the world?" *And why do you want to leave me?*

She blinks. "I don't want to."

"Well, you could've fooled me."

"I don't want to go, but I have to." Her voice is calm, resigned.

"Not if you can convince your mother that—"

"Abe, this is my boat ride. My way out."

Her boat ride! Of course. How did I miss that? The only way to get from London to New York in 1888 is by boat. It's exactly what she needs to break free. In which case she won't need the American cure—she'll be back in Fort Pippin and her vision will be restored.

She finds my hand. "You know I'd try to stay if I thought I could help you save someone. But I can't. Not when I'm like this. Blind."

"Don't worry about me, Mitz." I try to sound unruffled. "You need to go. I get it now."

"And you need to stop someone from dying. Soon."

"Yeah," I say, but I'm shaking my head. Let's face it, I keep messing up my chances to save someone. I'm always too late or too early, or I go down wrong alleys. I need to start preparing myself for being stuck here. Alone.

17

Time hurtles forward when your whole life is about to change. I sprint from work to the tenement and back to work. In a whir, I take the Kraskovs to pawn off their belongings, and I help them pack up their meager lives. I try to avoid the hateful headlines and the cold whispers, but they find me anyway. I get too little time with Mitzy, and no time alone with her. Then the day arrives. The day to say goodbye.

Now we're on the platform at the Fenchurch Street station, where the Kraskovs will catch a train to the shipping docks in Liverpool. It's a long ride, two hundred miles, but nothing compared to the trip across the Atlantic.

Mitzy and I stand off to one side while Duvid and Mrs. Kraskov wait closer to the tracks, watching their bags. Mrs. Kraskov is rubbing the finger where her wedding band used to be. Duvid is scratching the side of his leg where the rock pelted him. Something had to be done, so here we are.

The black giants idling on the tracks fill the station with the stink of coal smoke. It smells of something else too. Of forever, I think. I raise my head to the mocking morning sunlight that pours through the arched glass ceiling. I want to shut it all out. I want to run away. I want to break free.

"Let's go over the plan again," Mitzy says. "Plan B."

"Fine," I sigh. "When you get to New York, if you end up staying there—"

"If I end up stuck there, you mean. Stuck in 1888."

"Yeah." A man with a watch chain and top hat brushes past us, close enough for me to catch the spice of his pipe smoke. "If you get stuck in New York, write me. And if I'm still here, I'll try to...I'll try talking my mother into..."

"You and your mother will join us in Brooklyn."

"Yeah, we'll join. If we can. We're even poorer than you, y'know, but we'll join if we can."

"You can. You will," she commands. "If it even comes to that. Which I hope and pray it doesn't."

"Me too."

We're quiet for a few minutes. A man in a conductor's uniform whistles as he hustles by. A boy in crisp short pants and slicked-back hair skips past. A cotton-ball cloud dances over the glass ceiling. Now I think I hear Mrs. Kraskov calling us, but I don't look up to check. I don't want to know.

Mitzy turns her ear toward the tracks. "That's Mama. It's time." She looks surprised somehow, like she'd thought she could go to New York and stay here too, like the panic I've been feeling all along is finally hitting her.

"You have the address, right?" she whispers.

I pat my vest pocket. "Right here."

"Good." Mitzy is trying to be strong, but her voice wobbles. "Hold on to it, just in case."

"I will."

I glance up at the big clock. People begin forming a line at the train door. This is it. It's time.

I take Mitzy's arm and start guiding her to her mother. I don't say anything because there's nothing to say. No, that's not true. There are a thousand things to say. A hundred thousand. But I don't feel like talking.

Because what if plan A *and* plan B fail? I mean, if we both end up stuck in 1888, wouldn't it be better to be stuck here together? No, it wouldn't. Mitzy's family isn't safe here in Whitechapel. Not with the Ripper at large and people blaming the Jews.

The train doors pop open with a squeal. Last-minute travelers come scurrying onto the platform. Mrs. Kraskov waves to me. A woman holding a lapdog rushes by. This is it. Goodbye.

We reach Duvid and Mrs. Kraskov, and I help them carry their belongings to the end of the passenger line. The Kraskovs don't own much, so their bags feel light, practically empty, kind of like the hole forming in my chest.

The line moves way too fast, and suddenly Duvid is shaking my hand and picking up the bags. Something flickers in his eyes. Disappointment maybe, or surrender. There he goes now, boarding the train, the train that will take the three of them away from me. I turn to look at Mitzy one last time.

Then something funny happens.

The smell in the station, the burning coal smell, changes to something else. Something like cloves, or maybe it's licorice. Now I feel heavy. Heavy and off. Then everything goes black.

18

The lights go back on, dimly. I need a minute to adjust to the murk. I blink, squint, open my eyes wide, waiting for the sights and smells of the train station to return, waiting to say goodbye to Mitzy. But that's not where I am, or when I am.

I'm standing outside the old Fort Pippin post office building. There's Blue Marble Novelties, the Loose Goose Café, and at the top, Zinnia's place with a CLOSED sign in the window.

I'm home!

I came back the moment Duvid Kraskov boarded the train. So whatever help I gave him in escaping London, it must have saved his life, must have freed him from the attacks in Whitechapel. It actually worked. Zinnia's prediction for me was real.

"Which means her prediction for Mitzy is real too." I don't realize I'm speaking my thoughts out loud until a little old lady who's walking a black chihuahua stops and looks up at me.

"What's that, young man?" she asks.

"Oh, sorry." I hold my hands up. "I...sorry, nothing."

She nods and moves on.

Closing my eyes, I listen to the traffic noises, the cars and the skateboards, the boom box at the corner, a whistle. I breathe in the smell of Antonio's Pizza across the street, and above that, clean air. I look down at my jeans and my sneakers. I really am back. Back in Fort Pippin. Back in the twenty-first century. Home. Mitzy will be coming home too...but when?

"Glory days, well they'll pass you by," sings a man walking in my direction, his hands to his earphones. "Glory days."

"Excuse me," I say. He must have the volume cranked because he doesn't hear me. "Excuse me?" I say louder.

He stops, pulls out one ear bud, hoists his backpack a little higher on his shoulder, scratches his beard. "Whatcha got?" he asks, which I guess is hipster talk for *can I help you?*

Yes, I want to answer. *You can help me figure out how long I've been gone through the wormhole.* But I can't ask that—it sounds insane. Instead, I say, "Do you know what time it is?"

His eyebrows rise, like he's surprised to hear such a question. "Sure thing," he says, reaching into his jeans pocket. "Nice to know there are still some kids who aren't glued to their phones."

My cell phone—of course. I could've just reached into my own jeans pocket and looked up the time and date on my own phone…if it's still charged, that is. But no, the battery can't still be running. I've been gone way too long for that.

"It's 3:47," the man says.

I want to ask him what date it is, but that feels weird, so I don't. "Great, thanks."

"No problem." He puts his ear bud back in and heads on his way.

I glance around to see if there are any missing persons' posters on streetlights or store windows, but there aren't. Well, the police—maybe even the FBI—are surely searching for us. I wonder what our parents are going through, and how mine will react when I walk through the door this afternoon. How long *has* it been?

"Well then." I pull my phone out. "I might as well give it a try."

I press the power button, and the phone actually turns on. Not only that, it's at 88 percent. But that's not the half of it. It's still September 22—still National Elephant Appreciation Day, the same day I first left here for London. I was only gone for about twenty minutes. Feels like years. Decades.

"Uff." Someone bangs into me from behind, someone

with sharp elbows and a choice vocabulary. I turn around to get a look at whoever wasn't watching where they were going.

It's Mitzy!

Mitzy is back. She's breathing hard, and her face is on the green side, but otherwise she looks the way she's supposed to, with her blue hair glinting off the sunlight and her wrist bangles shivering down her arm. I'm so incredibly relieved. And yet...

Did she bump into me because she couldn't see me? Is she still blind?

"M-Mitzy?" I stammer.

She doesn't reply. She just stares blankly at the air, at nothing.

"It's me. Abe."

"Abe, where...?" Now her eyes mist over. She squeezes them shut, but the tears leak out. The wail that escapes her lips fractures my heart.

"Mitzy, no." My voice cracks right along with my heart.

"It's no good." She shudders. "It's still all black."

"I'm sorry. I'm so sorry." I touch her arm, but she steps away from me. She steps away from me and buries her face in her hands. I watch her cry and cry, and it feels like another decade passes until her tears ebb.

When she finally lowers her hands, she looks different. Partly because her face is swollen from crying. Partly because she can't stop blinking. And partly because she's—I'm not sure, but it seems like she's looking straight into my eyes. Like she can...

"Mitzy?"

"I can see! I can see!" She twirls around to get a 360-view of downtown. "I couldn't at first, but now I can."

"Thank God." My voice still splinters a little, but my heart is gluing itself back together. I want to hug her, but I don't know if that's okay in this here and now. I don't know why she backed away from me when I touched her a minute ago. I don't know anything.

"And I'm back!" she gushes, wiping her eyes. "I came back!"

"Home at last," I say, but she's not listening. She's talking to herself, not to me. Maybe she doesn't remember what we went through together, what we were to each other back then and there. Maybe I'm nothing to her all over again.

Or wait, maybe she's just having a little amnesia. Maybe she had a rough trip through the wormhole, or on the boat ride. Maybe there's still hope.

"So how did it happen, your coming back?" I ask.

"I…" she starts, but she's too busy admiring the shops, the traffic, the potholes. "I, um…hmm?"

"You were about to tell me how it went."

"Oh yeah. I, we…" She stops and scratches her elbow, like she's having a hard time answering my question. "Weird, I don't remember saying goodbye to you. I remember being with you at the station, and getting on the train, but not, y'know, waving goodbye or anything."

I nod. "That's because I beamed out right before you boarded. Right after Duvid got on the train."

"I guess that makes sense," she says, still looking a little puzzled. "Anyway, we had a long ride to Liverpool—the train was constantly stopping dead on the tracks. Then we spent the night at some really awful fleabag inn. The next day we boarded the ship, which, believe me, was no Carnival Cruise. And then…" Her voice trails off.

"And then?" I urge.

"And I don't know after that." She shifts her weight from one foot to the other, which has the effect of pushing her another half-step away from me. "I remember the ship start-ing to move. I remember my stomach starting to churn." Her forehead wrinkles. "I must've blacked out after that, because next thing I know, I'm mowing you down. Sorry, by the way."

"It's okay." *You can mow me down anytime, anytime at all.*

"What about you?" she asks. "If you beamed out at the train station, you must've come home a couple of days ago, right?"

I shake my head. "I got here about ten minutes before you did."

"Ten? Minutes?"

"Yeah, weird timing."

"Mmm." She narrows her eyes. "Speaking of timing, what day is it?"

"The same day we left. We were only gone a few minutes."

"What?" Her eyes grow wide. "No way."

"I know. It's a good thing, though. This way, no one here had to worry about us, y'know?"

"Yeah, I guess. Yeah." She sounds kind of distracted, like maybe she's looking straight through me again, like nothing has changed since I nodded to her on the memorial bench, since I chalked it up to another rotten day. Any second now, she's going to go on her way. Our odyssey will be over. We'll go back to not talking, to being practically strangers.

I'm not ready for that, not yet. I need her to stay a little longer, talk to me a while more. If only I could think of something clever to say, then maybe she'd hang out. Maybe she'd stand here on the sidewalk with me for a few more minutes and let me believe she still—even just a little bit—cares.

A motorcycle peels past, and I glance up at the driver, a guy in a weathered leather jacket and reflective shades, a guy who has cool written all over him. If I were half as boss as this guy, or even a quarter, I could find a way to keep her here, but I'm not. I can't think of a single thing. It's over.

But wait, hold on here. While I'm looking up, while I'm searching for the right words, I notice something. The arts cinema down the block. The marquee says: TODAY'S MATI-NEE—THE LITTLE PRINCE. Bingo.

"Hey, look what's playing." I tip my head toward the cinema. She follows my gaze. "We should, like." I scratch my head. "Maybe we should see it sometime."

"No. No thanks."

She doesn't even have to stop to think about it. It's a full-stop no.

"I…oh." I want to dissolve into the ground or evaporate into thin air, anything to escape the scorching bite of Mitzy's brush-off. The sudden hush between us roars in my ears. If every day in Whitechapel felt like a month, well, every second of this silence feels like a year. "Y-yeah," I falter. "Anyway, I should, um, get going."

"I've seen it. They do the story like a flashback." She wrinkles her nose. "And they add another main character. Strays too much from the original story."

"Okay, just a thought." I'm dying here.

"Besides, I've done enough sitting for a while." She shades her eyes with her hand. "Way more than twenty minutes, right?"

"Right." I try to smile, but I have the feeling it comes out as a grimace. I wish she'd stop making up excuses. I wish she'd let me drag my miserable tail home.

"I'm just gonna stretch my legs for a while now," she says.

This is my cue to step aside so she can beat a path away from me, so I do.

She nods but doesn't walk away yet. "Abe?"

"Mmm hmm?"

"Are you gonna tell anyone about this?"

Which just goes to show how little she knows me. Who am I supposed to tell—the buddies I don't have? The sister who already thinks I'm a geek? "Probably not. You?"

"I think…" She looks up at the sky. "I think I'd rather pull out my toenails than subject myself to that."

I try the smiling thing again. Not sure I do any better on the second shot. "Our little secret then."

"Actually, I'm gonna try to forget the whole thing ever happened. Just like Maya and Asher are probably doing."

So. No mutual secret. No shared memory. Tonight when I replay everything in my mind, the thoughts will be mine alone. I'm the only one who will ever relive it.

"But I do want to find out if that stuff really happened," she says. "Like, if they blamed the kosher butchers and ran riots and stuff."

I nod. "Maybe I'll write a story about it."

"That's a good idea. You should do it as soon as you get home, while it's still fresh." She's sending me back to my little saltbox of monotony, because obviously I'm not going anywhere with her.

"Right, yeah." I clear my throat. "Well, have a good walk home."

She pokes her tongue into her cheek. "Oh, I'm not going home yet. I'm gonna take a loop around the track at school."

Wait, what? She's going to walk the track, *my* track, the one she knows I take every morning?

"Feel like coming along?" she asks. I don't realize I'm standing here like an idiot without answering. Not until she speaks again. "Just, y'know, to see what it's like this time of day. Unless two's a crowd."

"No, no, that's great. Two is, yeah, great."

She turns in the direction of the crosswalk, but I'm still frozen—classic geek move.

"Coming?" she says.

"Uh, yeah."

I join her at the curb, and a bus stops to let us cross. I feel like the whole world is watching us, like I *want* the whole world to watch us. To watch me and Mitzy walking together, talking together, being together. I have the feeling I'm grinning like a fool.

We get to the opposite sidewalk and start walking in the direction of school. Was it really just an hour ago that I passed her on the memorial bench, that she ignored me, that I chalked it up to another rotten day?

"I was thinking." She slips her hand in mine.

Whoa. She's holding my hand. Mitzy Singer is holding my hand in this here and now. The impossible has happened—again. "Mm-hmm?" I manage.

"Maybe you can teach me how to let ideas in."

I laugh. There's nothing to teach, nothing to learn. It just happens when it wants to happen. But I don't say that. Instead, I say, "And maybe you can teach me how to clear my mind."

"Okay, yeah. It might take some time, though."

"I was hoping you'd say that."

She squints over at me. Glides her thumb over mine. Smiles.

We walk on, and I wonder what story we'll make together next.

Author's Note

At the time of the Ripper spree, more than 100,000 Jews lived in the East End of London. Many of them were recent immigrants who were fleeing violent anti-Semitism in Eastern Europe. Some Londoners had already begun to accuse the Jews of stealing jobs and housing from the English. Clearly, anti-Semitism was rife in the city by the time the Ripper struck.

Soon after the Ripper's first murder in 1888, people started blaming the Jews. As the *East London Observer* wrote in September of that year, "...in several quarters of East London the crowds who had assembled in the streets... began to threaten and abuse such unfortunate Hebrews... It was repeatedly asserted that no Englishman could have perpetrated such a horrible crime..."

One anti-Semitic theory centered on the idea that the Ripper was a *shochet*, or Jewish ritual slaughterer. London's divisional surgeon of police, George Baxter Phillips, stated that the Ripper's weapon "must have been a very sharp knife with a thin blade, from six to eight inches in length, probably longer. It could not have been a bayonet or a sword bayonet. The knife might have been one such as a slaughterer uses, well ground down. I think the knives used by cobblers would not have been long enough. There were indications of anatomical knowledge displayed by the person..."

The Juwes are not the men that will be blamed for nothing. This strange graffiti, appearing on the night that the Ripper struck twice, bolstered the accusations against the Jews. London's Metropolitan Police Commissioner ordered the graffiti removed, claiming it would provoke violence against the Jews if it remained. However, his men refused to carry out the order, saying that it would obliterate important evidence, so the commissioner erased it himself.

City divisional surgeon Dr. Gordon Browne eventually examined a selection of *shochet* knives to see if they resembled the probable murder weapon. An 1888 *Jewish Chronicle* article, quoted later in London's *The Star* in October 1888, stated: "We are authorised by Dr. Gordon Browne...to state, with reference to a suggestion that the City and Whitechapel murders were the work of a Jewish slaughterer, that he has examined the knives...and he is thoroughly satisfied that none of them could have been used."

Elizabeth Stride, the first victim on the night of September 30, was found by Louis Diemschutz, the steward of the largely Jewish International Working Men's Educational Club. Catherine Eddowes, the second victim that night, was discovered by a police constable in Mitre Square. Six weeks later, Mary Jane Kelly was found in her apartment by her landlord while trying to collect rent.

George Hutchinson, a friend of Mary Jane's, claimed that he saw her and a man go to her apartment on the night of the murder. Hutchinson later told the police that "the man was Jewish-looking." According to reports at the time, the police put great stock in Hutchinson's description of the Ripper.

Acknowledgements

I'd like to thank editor extraordinaire Jaynie Royal for helping me make this story the best it could be. Thanks also to Sam Flaster for his eagle eyes and his spot-on sensibilities. I'm grateful for the informational resource casebook.org, as well.